Someone is lying to Jackie. . .but how can she be sure who?

"Melanie cannot be trusted," Reed said quietly. "She lies until she no longer recognizes the truth."

"Tell me, what's the truth about you two?" Jackie crossed her arms and glared at him accusingly. "Why would Melanie leave a message if you two weren't involved?"

"Jackie," he began, stepping toward her.

She backed up, shaking her head. "Don't touch me."

"Please, believe me," he pleaded. "I would never do anything to hurt you."

Jackie lifted her chin. "Do you tell her the same thing?"

"No, honey. . ."

She waved her hands in front of her. "Don't call me honey. Just take me home."

DIANN MILLS lives in Houston, Texas, with her husband Dean. They have four adult sons. She wrote from the time she could hold a pencil but not seriously until God made it clear that she should write for Him. After three years of serious writing, her first book *Rehoboth* won favorite **Heartsong Presents** historical for 1998. Other publishing credits include magazine articles and short stories, devotionals, poetry, and internal writing for her church. She is an active church choir member, leads a ladies' Bible study, and is a church librarian.

Books by DiAnn Mills

HEARTSONG PRESENTS
HP291—Rehoboth
HP322—Country Charm
HP374—The Last Cotillion
HP394—Equestrian Charm

The Color of Love

DiAnn G. Mills

Heartsong Presents

I dedicate this book to my sister-in-law, Roberta Morgan. Thanks for your help and encouragement. I also wish to acknowledge David and Kay Egert for their invaluable research assistance.

This story belongs to Brett.

A note from the author:
I love to hear from my readers! You may correspond with me by writing:
DiAnn Mills
Author Relations
PO Box 719
Uhrichsville, OH 44683

ISBN 1-58660-149-0

THE COLOR OF LOVE

Cover illustration by Ron Hall.

PRINTED IN THE U.S.A.

prologue

Reed meticulously folded the piece of delicate stationery and eased it back into the embossed envelope. He turned it over in the palm of his hand and read his name across the middle. Painstakingly, his forefinger brushed across the letters as though erasing every word carefully penned inside. His movements were slow and deliberate, but his heart raced, then slowed as reality gradually overwhelmed him.

Melanie. The mention of her name sounded musical, like her laughter—contagious laughter that now rose higher and higher, echoing in a thousand voices, all mocking him. He'd been warned it would never work, but he refused to believe it. He loved her with every breath that poured from his being. Yes, he loved her more than life, and he'd gladly sell his soul to the devil to have her back again.

In his heart, he knew God forbid such thoughts, but he didn't care. Melanie had abandoned him, and her final words—the awful truth that he'd lived with every day of his life had now taken its final toll.

They would have been married in three weeks. Maybe she felt premarital jitters. Of course, that must be it. Within minutes he'd hear the phone ring, and she would be sobbing, apologizing for breaking his heart, declaring she didn't mean a word of it.

Except Reed knew the truth; deep down he'd known it all along from the way she sometimes looked at him, curious, frightened, and, yes, repulsed. But when he questioned her, she denied any inner turmoil. He understood far more than she could ever imagine, but that didn't change a thing.

Melanie had left Toledo for good; at least, that's what her note said. She didn't need to worry about him chasing her to Chicago. He'd honor her decision. Why make things more uncomfortable? Poor girl, he knew this had been hard for her. Reed shook his head, as though dispelling her words that rolled around in his mind like misguided marbles.

"I realize now I can't marry a man of mixed race," she'd written. "I don't know what would happen to our children, and, Reed, I want children. My parents feel this is for the best. I'm sorry; I didn't mean to hurt you."

He thought they had gone far beyond those considerations. He remembered the late-night talks discussing the obvious issues of their relationship. Melanie had vowed her love; nothing could ever separate them.

Still grasping the envelope in his fist, Reed gingerly picked up their engagement picture. They both looked so happy, and he recalled the photographer teasing Melanie about her giggles.

His fingers tightened around the frame. He wanted to smash the picture into pieces, but he couldn't bring himself to destroy it. He didn't want to shatter her memory. Not just yet. Gently, he laid it upside down, burying it with forgotten promises.

Why had he swallowed the God stuff from his adopted parents? Lies, nothing but lies. A God who loved and cared for him? Impossible. He didn't fit anywhere, and all anyone needed to do was look at his face.

Reed had no race to call his own. In his mind, he existed as a castoff from society, a leper of color. Neither blacks nor whites wanted him dating their daughters. Nothing to call his own. Even his parents were different from him with their milky-white complexions and straight hair. Why had they adopted him? For that matter, why would anyone want someone of mixed race? All the talk of love and acceptance meant nothing. How could he ever trust anyone again?

Reed slammed his fist onto the dresser top. Hot, stinging tears poured from his eyes. *Why, God? Why?*

one

"Hey, Reed, you joining us for lunch?" Nathan Bennett asked, sticking his balding head inside the plush office of one of General Motor's top engineers.

Reed raised a finger from his computer, signaling a moment's concentration. He zoomed in on a three-dimensional layout of a future model, carefully studying a particular feature. "Yes!" he shouted, feeling a sense of victory wash over him.

"And what is so great?" Nathan asked, obviously interested.

"Oh, I finally figured out the problem with that new model's interior door design," Reed replied, leaning back in his black leather chair.

"The safety feature?" When Reed nodded, Nathan continued. "Good, we can celebrate over lunch. You can buy."

Reed noted the challenge in Nathan's dark blue eyes. "But I'm the genius." Reed wove his fingers behind his neck. "Don't you want to rub shoulders with the elite?"

"No, just fill my empty belly."

"Okay, okay." Reed feigned annoyance. "Where are you guys going?"

"Pizza. It's Friday, you know."

Reed grinned. "All right, I'll meet you there. I've got to stop at the bank first. In fact," he glanced at his watch, "I'll go now and meet you there."

"Get plenty of cash for lunch," Nathan called from the doorway as he disappeared down the hall.

Reed E-mailed the design engineer about his findings before logging off the computer. *God is good,* he thought with satisfaction. Whistling, he exited the office and made

7

his way to the elevators. He felt proud to be a part of General Motors, and his career had certainly escalated in the past eight years.

Outside, his red Blazer glistened in the sun, thanks to his fastidious care. He'd spent all last Saturday afternoon waxing it, and luckily the weather had cooperated. A few moments later, he drove down Alexis Avenue toward Lewis Street.

Swinging into the bank parking lot, Reed hurried into the building where a matronly receptionist greeted him.

"Can you direct me to the loan department?" he asked politely.

"Do you have an appointment?" the prim woman inquired with a professional smile.

"No, just interested in securing some information."

"Their offices are down the hall to the right." She pointed with a perfectly manicured nail, then glanced at a small clock on her narrow desk. "I'm not sure if anyone is back there or not; it's almost noon."

Reed thanked her and headed down the hallway. He'd done a thorough search on-line and found that this bank now offered the best rates on new home construction loans. He passed a line of desks until he reached a glass-enclosed office marked *Jackie E. Mason, Consumer Loans*. With the office empty but the door open, he chose to linger, hoping someone might appear.

"May I help you?" a female voice asked pleasantly.

Reed turned to face a lovely, olive-skinned young woman. For a moment, he felt himself taken back with the sweet sound of her voice and the intensity of her huge hazel eyes. "Yes, I'm looking for someone in the real estate loan department."

"I'm Jackie Mason. How can I help you?" She reached out to shake his hand, and he couldn't help but notice she didn't wear a wedding or engagement ring.

He wet his lips, thoroughly distracted. "I'd like to discuss a home loan."

"New or pre-owned?" she inquired.

"New," he replied.

"If you'll step into my office, I'll put together a packet of information for you." She ushered him inside.

Before Reed could explain he most likely had obtained enough data from their website, she pulled a brown manila envelope from inside her desk. He seated himself in one of two turquoise chairs across from her and attempted to calm his nerves, but these feelings were nothing new. Every woman made him feel uneasy. . .uncomfortable. Thoughts of Melanie still haunted him. He wished the loan officer had been a man—certainly not a woman as captivating as the lovely lady before him.

He shifted before speaking. "Ms. Mason. . ." Reed slowly exhaled. "I've done my homework, and I see your bank offers the best rates on new constructions."

"That we do," she said proudly, with a slight upturn of her lips. She handed him the envelope. "This gives specific information about our home loans, but we need you to complete an application before we go any further."

"May I have one?"

"Of course." Pulling a home loan application from a file inside her desk, she handed it to him. "If you haven't completed one of these before, they are quite lengthy and involved."

Reed leafed through the pages. "This will be a whole new experience. Do you want my blood type, too?" He attempted a faint grin.

She returned the gesture. "No, but we are a stickler for account numbers."

"I figured that. I'll get right on it after lunch."

"Would you like to schedule an appointment?"

He glanced up into a pair of arresting eyes. They were green, brown, and gold—all swirled together. "Yes, of course," he managed.

She opened an appointment book. "I have a two o'clock slot available today. Would you be able to finish the form by then?"

Reed considered his afternoon schedule. "Yes, I have my financial information with me. Two o'clock is fine."

"Good, I appreciate your flexibility." She brushed back long, dark curly hair from the shoulder of her navy blue suit. "And your name?"

"Reed Parker."

Ms. Mason penned in his information. "All right, Mr. Parker. I'll see you this afternoon." She smiled warmly, and he noted a little dimple in her chin.

"Thank you for your help." He stood and shook her extended hand.

All the way to meet his friends, he thought about the attractive young woman, her enchanting eyes, dark curly hair, and olive skin. He wondered if she might be. . .

Don't even think it, Reed admonished himself. *No point wasting time and energy contemplating something that won't ever happen.* He shook his head, realizing he had a difficult enough time talking to female coworkers. . .best leave things alone.

Inside the lively restaurant, Nathan and another engineer, Brad Simmons, motioned to Reed. He liked this place—colorfully decorated in all sorts of mismatched antique road signs and pictures attached to barn siding walls. The waitresses and waiters wore bib overalls, blue-and-white striped shirts, red bandannas, and train conductors' caps. The food was the best part and they served it in generous portions, which usually edged him toward an afternoon nap. He saw his friends had water waiting for him on the faux walnut table.

"We haven't ordered yet," Nathan said. "Sure didn't take you long."

"Ah, you know how it is when you have clout. I asked for a couple of mil on my signature and they wrote out a check," he replied soberly.

"Right." Brad chuckled. He was a square-faced man who had a knack of consuming more food than the other two. "With your expertise, maybe you can get our waitress's attention."

"Perhaps." Reed gave a wry grin, his typical noncommittal

response. "I'll be on the lookout."

"So, are you going ahead with the house plans?" Nathan asked.

"Yeah, I've been designing this thing for the past couple years. Might as well see what it looks like."

"Oh, great," Nathan moaned. "Kathi's been pestering me to get her and the baby out of the apartment. One word about this, and I'm sunk. She already thinks you're the perfect man."

Reed recalled the many times Nathan's wife had attempted to fix him up with her girlfriends, but he always graciously declined. Although Nathan and Kathi had known Melanie and knew the story behind the breakup, he found it easier to say he wasn't interested than risk becoming involved. "She thinks I'm wonderful because I have manners and class," he pointed out. "And those attributes make me a saint."

Before Nathan had an opportunity to reply above the roar of Brad's laughter, their waitress arrived.

❧

Jackie followed the hostess to a booth. It worried her a little that Shanna hadn't arrived, especially since she had a doctor's appointment prior to their arranged luncheon. She wished her sister carried a cell phone, but Jeff didn't make enough money to warrant what he considered a "luxury item." Still, with his wife eight months pregnant, extra precautions sounded like a necessity to Jackie.

Twisting her watch into view, she contemplated phoning her brother-in-law at his office. She'd wait a few more minutes, understanding the call would alarm him. Allowing her mind to drift back to the handsome man who approached her desk shortly before noon, she submerged herself in thoughts of Reed Parker. Shy and quiet, he'd impressed her with his polite mannerisms, except he did seem rather uncomfortable.

Jackie pondered Reed for another moment. He had an excellent build, like an athlete—broad shoulders, trim waist, and his clothes hung well—khaki pants and a hunter green knit shirt. Not that a man's dress meant much to her, but in Reed's case, it merely accented his good looks. She didn't know which she appreciated more, the smile lighting up his face or the soft brown eyes. Upon further thought, his eyes projected a rather sad mien. She smiled at her own reflections. Normally she didn't spend this much time evaluating the bank's customers, but somehow he seemed different.

Lord, I don't usually react like this. Are You trying to tell me something? I thought You wanted me to remain single, devoting my life to my career and helping Mom and Dad with all the kids.

A man hovered over her table, interrupting her musings. He was wearing a dirty shirt and sporting a day's growth of beard, and she wondered what he wanted.

"You sure are pretty," he said, displaying a mouth full of yellow, broken teeth. "Why don't I set down and keep you company?"

Jackie caught her breath. "I'm waiting for someone," she stated firmly.

He looked back at a table full of the same type of fellows and nodded knowingly. "No, I don't think so. You've been here awhile."

"Sir, I appreciate the offer, but I'd prefer to be left alone." She felt more than slightly irritated.

"I'll just sit here until your friend comes." He chuckled, and bent to scoot into the booth opposite her.

"Please," she insisted, grabbing her purse with the intention of leaving. She didn't need his aggravation.

"Hi, Jackie, sorry I'm late."

Surprised, her gaze flew to Reed's face as he stood beside the intruder.

"Have you been waiting long?" he asked with a smile she hadn't seen in their first meeting. He cast a challenging look at the bearded man. "Do you need something?"

The man shrugged his shoulders. "No," he mumbled.

"Good. May I join the lady now?"

Jackie watched the man return to his table. "Thank you so much," she whispered. "My sister planned to meet me here for lunch, but she hasn't arrived yet."

"You're welcome, and I apologize for barging over here. I'm sure you're more than capable of handling yourself." He sounded a bit awkward.

She appreciated his concern and chivalry. "Well, most of the time. You rescued me from a very unpleasant situation." She smiled in a way that she hoped would relax him.

"Would you like to join me and my friends until your sister arrives?"

"Thank you, but I see she just walked in." Jackie waved toward the front entrance.

Reed sat until a pregnant young woman, one of Asian descent, made her way to the booth.

"Mr. Parker, this is my sister Shanna Robertson," Jackie introduced. "And Shanna, this is Reed Parker, a new friend."

He stood to greet the young woman. "It's a pleasure to meet you," he replied pleasantly, then nodded at Jackie. "Excuse me while I rejoin my friends." He stepped aside, allowing Shanna to sit across from her sister.

She glanced from Jackie to Reed. "Am I interrupting anything?" Shanna asked, a look of amusement in her brown eyes.

"Not at all." Jackie turned her attention back to Reed. "Thank you again, and I'll see you at two." She watched him join the other men, studying him for a brief moment longer.

"Oh, and who is he?" Shanna teased. "I haven't seen him before, and he's really good-looking."

Jackie tilted her head thoughtfully. "I met him less than an hour ago when he stopped into my department at the bank."

Shanna leaned across the booth. "Well, Sis, he certainly has made a big hit with you."

two

Reed avoided his friends' apparent gaping stares and slid back into the booth before biting into a thick slice of pepperoni and mushroom pizza. Knowing their inquisitive minds, he decided to say nothing about the incident with Jackie. Let them stew awhile. After all, he'd been the brunt of too many of their jokes.

"You're not getting off this easy," Brad said with a wry smile. "Are you going to explain what just happened?"

"Perhaps," Reed stated, purposely popping in a mouthful of hot cheese bread.

"No 'perhaps' about it," Nathan informed him. "We're your buds, and we didn't realize you were so good with the women, especially one that gorgeous."

Reed couldn't resist the urge to nettle them. "Oh, her? I hadn't noticed. Frankly, it seemed like the thing to do. Besides, she didn't look like she wanted that guy's attention."

Brad's green eyes narrowed. "Aw, come on," he said dryly. "And I thought you were shy. Have you been holding out on us?"

Reed shrugged off the question nonchalantly and took a long drink of water before replying. "Perhaps."

Brad cringed and breathed deeply, accenting his square shoulders, square face, and square body. "If I hear that word one more time, I'm going to ask *her* where you two met."

"Impatient, aren't we?" Reed lifted another slice of pizza from the plate to his mouth, slowly savoring every tasty morsel. "She's merely one of many."

Nathan chuckled. "You forget, pal, I've known you since high school. Try something else."

"Truthfully?" Reed asked. He leaned back to eye Nathan beside him, a slender man with a slight build, totally opposite

14

in appearance from Brad.

"Yeah," he replied. "And she's not your sister."

"She's a loan officer at the bank. Just met her, before I joined you two. Satisfied?"

Brad frowned. "No. You two seemed very friendly."

Reed raised his hands. "Honest truth. We've barely spoken, and only business."

Nathan leaned across the table, waving a slice of pizza at Reed. "So when are you going to see her again?"

"Two o'clock," he mumbled, and waited for the laughter to die down.

The truth known, Reed enjoyed talking with Jackie. Those eyes of hers. . .one look and he had drowned in them. He wondered if she always projected such a sweet personality. *No matter; forget it,* he ordered himself. *Don't build up your hopes. Women are all alike—can't trust them.*

But in his heart, Reed wanted to believe Jackie Mason was different. Thoughts of her leaped across his mind, reminding him of jumping hurdles during his college days. His insecurity about women was the obstacle—too high for him to even consider. Years had passed since a woman had affected him in quite the same way, and the momentary exhilaration felt foreign.

But for a brief lapse in time, he dared to dream.

From the corner of his eye, he stole a glance at her booth, farther down on the opposite side of the aisle. A waitress stood taking their order, but he thought Jackie looked his way. Slightly embarrassed, Reed hastily turned his attention back to Brad's latest rendition of his golf game.

Suddenly he remembered Jackie had introduced the Asian girl as her sister. Irritation crept over him. Did she think he was an idiot? Those two weren't any more sisters than Nathan and Brad were his brothers—unless adoption factored into it. Maybe he had more in common with Jackie than he originally thought.

～

At two o'clock, Jackie welcomed Reed into her office for the second time that day. As he sat down opposite her desk to conduct the interview, she gave him a sincere smile. "Thank you again, for coming to my aid today. I sincerely appreciate it."

"You're welcome," he replied, clearly flustered. "Glad I could help." He pulled the application form from his file folder and laid it before her.

Feeling awkward with her own reactions to the man seated across from her, she picked up the completed form and quickly scanned his information. Her gaze trailed to the section indicating his marital status—single. "So, you've already purchased three acres south of Bowling Green?" she asked, jotting down her notes on a legal pad.

"Yes," he replied, sitting rigid in the same chair he'd occupied previously.

She attempted to coax a smile from him—and succeeded. At last he showed signs of relaxing; she always prided herself in her ability to make potential clients feel comfortable. "I know the area; my parents live in the same vicinity. Very pretty country."

"I agree, just rural enough for privacy yet close to town, which is why I want to build there."

"We'd love to help you, Mr. Parker, but we can't promise anything. At this point we need to make the necessary credit inquiries."

"I understand."

His low, husky voice unnerved her. "Now, where is the land financed?"

"It's paid for."

"Oh, good. Have you contacted a builder?" She glanced up and met his soft brown gaze beneath a thick, veiled curtain. *Your lashes are entirely too long for a man, Mr. Parker. Most women would die for those eyes.*

"I've narrowed it down to one. He constructs quality homes and has an excellent reputation. But first things first. Right now I need to secure a loan." He settled back stiffly in his chair. "When should I call you again?"

She leafed through her opened planner. "You can call me

next Wednesday. I will have your credit report this afternoon, but I'm swamped Monday and Tuesday." She handed him her business card. "Here's my number."

"Thank you." He stood and stuck her card inside his folder. "I appreciate your time."

"You're quite welcome." She willed her fluttering heart to slow to a mere race.

Watching Reed exit down the hall until out of sight, Jackie wondered what had come over her. *I'm acting like a giddy teenager,* she scolded. *This isn't like me at all. Admittedly, he's good-looking and his shy temperament makes him. . . well, appealing.*

For a brief moment, she considered his nationality—his deeply tanned skin and sandy-colored short hair led her to believe he might be biracial. Jackie stiffened. *He probably knows his own race, though, which is far better than having no clue.* She grimaced. Feeling a twinge of remorse for her thoughts, she sighed. *Sorry, Lord, I know who I am in Your eyes and that's what really matters.*

Reed remained constantly on her mind throughout the afternoon. Jackie found it hard to concentrate on her work. She watched the clock, knowing that in a few short hours she could leave loan applications, anxious clients, and memories of Reed at the office.

Promptly at five o'clock, she locked her desk and files containing privy information. With the bank offering low interest rates on mortgage loans, she'd received a flood of calls. Normally she stayed until seven to work on the increasing number of applications, but not tonight. She felt exhausted. Management had been looking for someone to handle real estate loans so she could manage the commercial side of the business, but so far no one had been hired.

Snatching up a stack of papers, she stuffed them into her slim, navy blue briefcase. These really needed to be examined by Monday morning before the monthly board meeting. Mentally, she put aside Saturday night to work through them.

Stepping out into the warm spring afternoon, she made her

way to her silver metallic Camaro, glistening in the sunshine. It needed a good washing—something for Saturday morning before she took her brothers and sisters to the park. Remembering her commitment, she unarmed her car, dug through her purse for the cell phone, and punched in her parents' number while she slipped her key into the ignition.

After two rings, Nita Mason answered. Jackie pictured her short, round, white-headed mother bustling through the kitchen preparing dinner for her dad and six brothers and sisters.

"Hi, Mom."

"Hi, sweetie. Did you have a good day?" As always, her voice sounded cheery, optimistic.

"Great. What's for dinner?"

"Um, baked chicken, pasta salad, and whatever else I throw together." Nita laughed. "Would you like to join us?"

"You're tempting me, but I can't. I've got to clean my apartment. Are the kids planning on me taking them to the park tomorrow?"

"Yeah—sure of it. What time will you be here?"

"About one, right after lunch."

"Sounds good. Your dad plans to clean out the van when he gets home this evening. The new hydraulic lift was installed earlier in the week, and he swears the service technician left it filthier than when we took it in."

The two laughed, picturing the meticulous man complaining about his dirty vehicle. "All right. I'll see you tomorrow. . . Mom?"

"Hmm."

"Do you know a Parker family in the area?"

"As a matter of fact, I do. They are our age and go to our church. Why do you ask?"

"Do they have any kids?"

"Just one, a son who's about thirty-two or so."

Jackie felt her heart beat furiously. "Have you ever seen him?"

"No, but his mother talks about him all the time. You see, he's adopted, and we have lots in common."

Jackie smiled, thinking about her loving parents adopting eight hard-to-place children, from children with physical handicaps to a little sister with Down's syndrome. "Is his name Reed?"

"I believe so."

"I met him today, very nice man."

"According to his mom, he's handsome and extremely shy."

Jackie chuckled. "Same one. Thanks, Mom, I'll see you tomorrow."

"For lunch?"

"Okay, you twisted my arm."

Her mother's voice held a smile as she said, "And I'll let you tell me more about meeting Reed Parker."

three

Reed felt the wet, cold tongue of Yukon, his gray Siberian husky, lap his face. Feigning sleep, he hoped the pet would soon abandon his playful mood. But the dog had other ideas. Again, Yukon licked Reed's jaw, working his way up the side of Reed's cheek, across his ear, and up his hairline.

"You win," he groaned. "But I need to teach you to distinguish Saturday from the rest of the week."

The dog barked and with a lunge, he jumped up beside him. Placing his front paws on Reed's shoulder, Yukon nuzzled his head beneath the blanket and grasped it with his teeth, before pulling it to the end of the bed.

He shook his head. "No wonder I've never married. What woman would put up with you?" Yukon bounded up and rested his head under Reed's chin. "Or give me this much attention." He petted the dog fondly. "What do you say we head to the park this afternoon?"

Yukon peered into Reed's face, recognizing the word "park."

"This afternoon, not now. First I want to go over some designs on our new home. Maybe it will get my mind off a certain Miss Mason." The dog tilted his head, giving the impression of wanting more information. Reed chuckled and continued to stroke the soft, furry coat. "Oh, you'd like her, too. Beautiful and very sweet. Most likely out of my league, though. You know me, fella; don't do well with the ladies." He stared into the dog's blue eyes and paused, as though the animal might choose to respond. Yukon barked again. "Okay, I'm getting up. I understand—nature's calling."

After slipping into navy blue sweats and running shoes, Reed grabbed his keys while Yukon tugged successfully on a leash hanging from a peg near the kitchen door. Snapping it onto the collar, he unlocked the door and stepped out into the cool spring morning.

"I'll let you run free tonight at Mom and Dad's," he promised. "And as long as we're out there, we might as well check on our little piece of property."

Reed stretched out, and a short while later the two took off in a slow run—with Yukon now and then stopping to sniff beneath a tree.

Shortly after lunch, Reed packed up his Blazer for an afternoon at the park and the subsequent trip to his parents' home. If they hadn't viewed his land by now, he intended to take them there before dinner.

The day had warmed considerably so that his sweatshirt provided all the warmth he needed for the April day. With Yukon seated in the backseat, Reed eased out of his apartment complex parking lot and onto the street. The freeway in its symmetrically arched formations of concrete and stone led him out of Toledo into the suburb of Perrysburg—and to Providence Metro Park, nestled in the trees beside the Maumee River. *A picture-perfect day,* he surmised, as he swung his sports vehicle into a parking area. Patches of sunlight stole through the trees, weaving a weblike pattern through the branches and onto the grass. From his position, he saw nothing but budding, colorful plants and green—no one else to invade his private sanctuary. Yet he knew that illusion would be short-lived, for soon others would be enjoying the solitude and beauty.

Once he clicked Yukon's leash into place, he listened for the various birds calling and singing to each other. And, as he expected, he heard the distant sound of laughing children.

Reed spent the next hour tossing a rubber ball back and forth with his husky, realizing others wouldn't be fearful of a dog carrying something in its mouth. He prided himself in having a well-behaved, well-groomed pet. Many times, Yukon required only a single word of command.

"Come," Reed commanded, desiring a walk along the river. Leash in hand, the two made their way across the park.

The sound of laughter perked his attention. Glancing in

that direction, he watched a boy push a wheelchair frantically over the grass for another boy who hollered for him to hurry. Reed laughed out loud when the seated boy caught a Frisbee. Shouts of triumph lifted over the park.

Curious, he stepped closer to see who else was playing the game. An African-American youth shouted for the Frisbee to be returned while a Hispanic boy on crutches voiced something about fairness. The boy on crutches, who looked to be about twelve years old, was missing a leg. Off to the side near a picnic table, a girl watched the Frisbee game while a young woman knelt to talk to a small child in another wheelchair. When she stood, Reed thought she resembled Jackie Mason.

I can't get her off my mind, he told himself. *Can't possibly be the same person.* But still the thought lingered, so he and Yukon circled around the back of some trees to get a better view.

A slow grin spread across his face. It *was* Jackie. He couldn't quite decide whether to make himself known or not. Dressed in jeans and a lightweight green sweater, she continued to talk to the little girl in the wheelchair. Although Reed didn't hear the conversation, from the smile on Jackie's face he gathered she spoke tenderly to the child. Upon closer scrutiny, he saw the little girl displayed the characteristics of someone mentally challenged.

"A sled dog!" Another little girl pointed at Yukon.

Suddenly embarrassed at being discovered, Reed stepped into full view, keeping a firm hand on Yukon's leash.

A startled Jackie stood, then waved. "Hello. Didn't expect to see you here."

"It's one of our favorite spots. I mean, Yukon and me." He thought she looked lovelier than the day before—slightly flushed and definitely relaxed. A light breeze had whipped up the dark curls around her face, while the remainder of her hair had been fastened securely in a ponytail. Odd, he didn't remember she had such a slender figure.

"Yukon?" She moved closer. "That's your dog's name?"

He nodded. "Guess it doesn't show much ingenuity for a man working for General Motors."

Jackie laughed, and he enjoyed the musical lilt of the sound. "Is he friendly?"

"Yes, quite, in fact. Huskies are known for their gentleness and love of people." *Those eyes, those incredibly huge, hazel eyes.* He saw a spark of merriment in them—and a twinge of mischief.

"Would you mind showing him to the kids?"

"No, of course not."

Jackie turned to the boys still playing Frisbee. "Paul, Joey, Alex, Bud, come here. I have someone I want you to meet."

Within moments the four boys appeared. The eldest, an African-American youth, scowled until he saw the dog.

"Kids, this is Mr. Parker, a friend of mine."

"Reed," he corrected. He shook hands with the four boys and listened to them admire his dog.

"Wow, what a great-looking husky," one of the boys stated. "Can I pet him?"

"Sure, but let's make proper introductions first," Reed replied. Yukon stood obediently at his side with the rubber ball firmly planted in his mouth. Reed took the ball and nodded at the boys. "Paul?" he asked of the eldest.

"Right."

"Okay. Yukon, this is Paul. He'd like to get to know you." Glancing up at the youth, Reed smiled. "Let him smell your hands. Good. Now you can pet him."

Paul bent to stroke the animal's head. A few moments later, Reed introduced the other boys. Joey walked on crutches, but inched closer to pat the dog's head. Alex appeared fearful. However, Bud, the boy in the wheelchair, instantly loved Yukon.

"Can I pet him, too?" a blond, little girl asked timidly.

"Of course," Reed replied.

Jackie placed her hands on the child's shoulders. "This is Olivia."

Reed nodded, thinking Olivia's smile could melt the

winter's snow. He whispered in his pet's ear. The dog walked over to the girl and lifted his paw to shake hands. Her brown eyes sparkled.

"We were just about ready to have a snack," Jackie said. "Would you and Yukon care to join us?"

He looked at his dog questioningly, as if anticipating a reply.

"Does he understand you?" Bud asked incredulously.

Reed grinned. He liked these kids. "He does comprehend a lot of the things I say. He's a smart dog, and I think he just senses my movements and actions."

"Are you going to stay?" Paul asked. "I forgot the lemonade, but we have plenty of water and a bunch of chocolate chip cookies. Our mom made 'em."

Reed lifted a brow. "Homemade?"

"Yeah," Paul replied with a nod.

"Can't refuse that, can we, fella?" He patted the dog. "But Yukon will pass on the cookies. He's on a special diet."

Olivia giggled, and again Reed felt impressed with the group.

"Paul, would you mind Lacy for a moment while I get the water bottles and cookies from the van?" Jackie asked.

The boy immediately went to Lacy's side and grasped the handles of the wheelchair.

"I haven't met Lacy," Reed said, looking at the little red-headed girl seated beside Jackie.

Jackie's gaze met his and he felt his heart take a flip. "Lacy's our resident angel," she claimed.

He walked over and bent to the child's eye level. Instantly he saw the seriousness of her retardation. "It's a pleasure to meet you, Miss Lacy," he said softly, remembering a time when he had volunteered with these type of children. Lacy made a laughing sound.

"She likes you," Olivia noted.

"I'm glad." He stood and faced Jackie. Suddenly, the familiar shyness seized him, and he couldn't think of a single thing to say.

"Would you mind giving me a hand with the food?" She

pulled keys from her jeans pocket.

Relieved, he turned to the boys. "Would you keep an eye on the dog for me?"

"Sure," they echoed.

A few moments later, Reed and Jackie strode toward a white van. He felt awkward—talking to her came easier with the kids around. "So, you do volunteer work, Ms. Mason?"

"No," she said with a soft laugh, "and it's Jackie. They are my brothers and sisters. We're all adopted."

Admiration wrapped a special warmth around his heart. "That's wonderful. I'm adopted, too, but there's just one of me. Of course, I was a handful."

"I believe our parents are acquainted," she said, wetting her lips. "I hope you don't mind, but when you said your parents lived near your property, I asked Mom if she knew them."

"And they do?"

"Yes. Small world, huh?"

"Yeah, guess so," he replied. "And I don't mind. . .about your asking."

By this time they were at the van. Jackie unlocked the side sliding door and pulled out a large, brown bag while Reed grabbed a box full of bottled water and cookies.

"Um, I smell the cookies," he said, as chocolate filled his nostrils and his mouth watered. "Those kids may be fighting me for them."

Smiling, she locked the van and they headed back to the group. While Jackie spread a plastic, green-checked tablecloth over the picnic table, Reed entertained the children with Yukon's tricks.

"Let's pray and eat," she called shortly afterward. "Paul, would you ask the blessing?"

The group quickly joined hands, with Reed grasping Lacy's on one side and Jackie's on the other.

"Lord, we've had a great day, and we now thank You for this food. Amen." Paul grinned. "He knows I love Mom's chocolate chip cookies."

Reed quietly observed the others—a bit amused at their

antics and a bit backward in his own response. They were obviously Christians, but they had to have strong faith to challenge the odds against them. He recalled his own parents discussing adopting more children, except he'd been such a terror that they'd decided against it.

Without warning, he felt very uncomfortable. He'd stumbled into their afternoon fun, and suddenly he found himself in the midst of it. He glanced at Lacy, still without a cookie or water. She wanted one and her blue eyes flooded with tears.

"Just one minute, angel," Jackie soothed as she helped the others.

"I'll feed her," Reed offered.

"Are you sure?" Jackie asked with a bit of hesitancy.

He stood from the picnic bench. "Yes, I can handle her just fine. Break off small pieces so she doesn't choke, right?"

Jackie smiled appreciatively, and it warmed his heart. *I could watch her all day and all night,* he thought as a slight blush colored her cheeks.

"Okay, angel girl," he said to Lacy. "Let's get you fixed up." He popped a little piece into her open mouth. "Chew it up real good. Wonderful. Now, here's another."

By the time he finished feeding Lacy two cookies, the other kids had taken Yukon to join in their games. He wiped the little girl's mouth and gave her another small sip of water.

"You're excellent with her," Jackie softly complimented.

"My pleasure," he replied, meeting her gaze. Hastily he glanced away. "I probably need to get going. Yukon and I don't want to get in your way."

"Oh, you're not. We've enjoyed every minute of it, and you kept this crew entertained for me."

He rose from kneeling in front of Lacy, not really wanting to leave but feeling he ought to go. "Thanks, Jackie, for a great afternoon."

"And thank you."

He paused, despising the awkwardness. "I'll tell the others good-bye and get my dog." His heart pounded hard against his chest. For a moment, he feared she could hear it. An incredible idea overtook him. "Would you like to go to lunch on Monday?"

Was it his imagination, or did her hazel eyes light up with pleasure?

"I'd love to," she instantly responded.

"Good. I'll call you Monday morning."

As he walked away, heading toward the others, he wished he could have said something more witty. . .clever. He liked Jackie. She had a gentleness about her and a way of organizing those kids so that her work almost looked easy. She assigned each child a job and they did it. *Not me, at that age,* he reminded himself. *I gave a whole new meaning to the word "rebellion."*

Reed noticed she recognized the strengths in her brothers and sisters and used those traits to encourage them. And he didn't doubt any of those boys could be a real handful, but they respected her.

He chuckled. For a guy who didn't want to be interested, he'd observed a lot about Jackie Mason.

four

Jackie stared at the gold and green marble desk clock before her. She'd arrived at the bank forty-five minutes early and still hadn't made a dent in her paperwork. She'd delegated as much of it as possible, but the secretaries already had their own jobs to do. At least she'd had the forethought to take some things home over the weekend.

Um, the weekend, she mused. Seeing Reed on Saturday had sent her soaring and dreaming the rest of the day and on through Sunday. *Such a sweet man—polite, understanding, excellent with the kids, especially Lacy.* She welcomed his shy, gentle character and the way he easily blushed. How refreshing from fighting off men with too many arms and inappropriate intentions. In fact, she'd all but given up on dating. Jackie much preferred a man to be attracted to her heart, her values, and her love for the Lord—rather than considering her a challenge to conquer.

I've become cynical, she told herself. *And I have no business thinking about Reed Parker, a customer of this bank.* But he had asked her out for lunch today, and with that recollection she smiled, despite the stack of applications and follow-ups on her desk.

She finished her second cup of coffee and decided to fill it one more time. She'd always been a morning person, but not today after spending half the night working at home. Standing, she took a deep breath and walked toward the break room.

Norman Timmons hovered over the coffeemaker as though watching it drip would speed up the process. He snapped his fingers, then pulled a white napkin from the counter to jot down whatever had entered his mind.

"Good morning, Norm," Jackie greeted, purposely adding

28

a cheery note to her voice.

"Morning. Have a good weekend?" Her boss stuck the napkin inside his jacket and smiled through perfectly capped teeth. Having recently completed the dental work, he tended to beam—a lot. Of course, if she'd just spent a fortune on cosmetic dentistry, she'd make sure people noticed, too. He lifted his head, and she noticed that his walnut-colored hairpiece looked a bit lopsided. Another recent addition. Biting back a chuckle, she forced herself to be courteous.

"Oh, my weekend went well," she replied, setting her cup beside his. "Busy, though. I tried to get ahead on the paperwork, but I never seemed to reach bottom." She laughed. "Typical Monday—I'm complaining."

Norm shared her mirth, opening his mouth wide. Avoiding his nerve-grating tactics, she stared at the slowly rising brew. "Must have been a hectic weekend if we're already on a second pot and the tellers aren't here yet."

"Yeah. You, me, and Wilson are the only ones floating around."

Wilson Anderson had been her supervisor before his promotion to vice president, sidestepping Norm. The two rarely saw eye-to-eye on anything, with Norm initiating the opposite view of Wilson no matter what the issue. Nevertheless, she missed her old boss, a godly man who cherished his wife and children.

Norm's gray eyes raked her up and down, his thoughts shouting louder than his green neon tie. "I went out Friday and Saturday night, so I'm nursing a bit of a hangover," he informed her.

She refused to comment on Norm's party life. It only encouraged him to boast of his lady friends. Instead, she wiped up a puddle of water around the coffeemaker.

"Did I offend you?" he asked, studying her face with feigned sophistication.

She shrugged. "I believe we have different tastes in entertainment, that's all." Her voice remained pleasant. He would not goad her today, no matter how hard he tried.

"Ah, yes. Your entertainment is sitting in an old pew, listening to someone drone on about God stuff."

Jackie didn't reply. The last time she tried to talk to Norm about God, he wrote her up. Later, after the offense had been noted in her employee file, he apologized, insisting they could discuss the whole matter over a business dinner. She politely declined. Lately his comments and insinuations bordered upon harassment, but she needed her job and he hadn't said or done anything inappropriate in front of others. So she listened to him talk, keeping quiet about his lifestyle and never asking for details. Norm Timmons was at the top of her prayer list. Because of her intense dislike for the man, she had to pray for her own attitude.

He inhaled deeply and folded his arms across his fleshy chest. "Well, I happen to think church is dull, but I'm never bored. It's the single life for me. Personally, I find the health club is the perfect place to meet babes."

Jackie swallowed a retort. His health club membership hadn't helped relieve the strain on his shirt buttons.

"Oh, look, the coffee's done," she announced, relieved to change the subject. She poured his first, then filled hers. Cup in hand, she elected to leave the break room. "Have a good day, Norm."

"Thanks." He paused. "I may have some good news for you about your workload dilemma."

Turning on her heel, she gave him her full attention.

"We've hired someone to take over the real estate department." He always referred to "we" when he wanted to infer the upper management consulted him before hiring needed personnel.

"Really?" Her eyes widened.

"Yes. You should be able to meet her around eleven today. She comes highly recommended from one of our branches in Chicago."

"Wonderful," Jackie breathed. Help at last. "What's her name?"

He flashed her a knowing smile. "Melanie Copeland." He

half closed his eyes dreamily. "She has excellent credentials."

Reed had been watching the time on his computer since he strolled into the office two hours ago. *Nine-thirty,* he read. *About the right time to call Jackie.* Whirling around in his chair, he picked up the phone and glanced at the slip of paper on his desk where he'd scribbled down her number at the bank.

Drumming his fingers on the desk, he leaned back in his chair and waited for the delicious sound of her voice. He'd already gone beyond his normal practice of leaving the female gender to themselves—or to some other guy. Everything about Jackie appealed to him, and it had been a long time since he'd felt like spending time with a lady.

"Hello, Jackie Mason's office."

"Good morning, this is Reed Parker." He smiled, imagining Jackie perfectly poised at her desk. She'd have her dark, curly hair pulled back from her face and her trim figure clothed professionally.

"A good Monday morning to you," she said softly. "So glad you called. You really made a hit with the kids on Saturday."

"Thanks, they were great. Your parents have done a wonderful job with them."

"I'll be sure to pass that on."

Reed hesitated, suddenly attacked by a case of nerves. "Would you still like to go to lunch?" His heart thumped wildly against his chest.

"Oh, yes, I have it written in my planner."

He grinned. "What time should I pick you up?"

"Probably twelve-thirty. Normally I go a little earlier, but the bank has hired a new employee to relieve some of my workload, and I'm supposed to meet with her around eleven. Anyway, I have no idea how long it will take."

"Twelve-thirty it is." He paused. "Let me give you my cell phone number in case something comes up."

"Good idea." He gave her the information. "Thanks. I'm looking forward to seeing you again."

"Yeah, me too. I mean, having lunch."

She laughed ever so lightly and he joined her.

"Guess I'll see you later."

"Bye." Reed replaced the phone and spun the chair around to his computer. The morning could not pass fast enough.

Shortly after eleven, Nathan called to see what he wanted to do for lunch.

"Got plans today, sorry."

"Anybody I know?" Nathan asked in his typical cheery voice.

Reed hesitated. He didn't want to lie to Nathan, but he'd never live it down if the man knew the truth.

"You've got a date," Nathan accused. "Well, I'll be. Is it the girl from the bank?"

Letting out a slow breath, Reed shook his head at his friend's perception. "Perhaps."

"Perhaps it is." He whistled. "What a way to start the week. Where are you taking her?"

Truthfully, Reed hadn't decided. "Not sure yet. The Oaken Bucket?"

"Whew, she rates. Are you ready for a woman in your life?"

Reed envisioned Nathan passing on the news. "I'm not sure. Do me a favor and keep this to yourself."

"Sure. How long since you've last seen someone?" Nathan's voiced softened in understanding.

"A long time. This is the first."

"Need a prayer?"

"As a matter of fact, I do."

"You got it. Hope it works out for the best."

"Thanks. I'll talk to you later." As Reed replaced the phone, he considered Nathan and Kathi's friendship. They'd stood by him when he turned his back on them and God. Then the accident. . . If it hadn't been for their faithfulness and prayers, he would have willfully died. In more ways than one.

Never going there again, he vowed. *Lost my mind, my faith, my heart, and nearly my life for a woman who didn't care.* A shiver raced up his spine, and he quickly dispelled it.

Fear did things like that to a man.

❧

Jackie sat at her desk and pressed the cap of the slim tube of lipstick until it clicked, then dropped it into her cosmetic bag. She felt a bit foolish feeling so excited about lunch with Reed, but a man hadn't spurred her interests in a long time. Feeling a hint of apprehension, she decided not to make more of this casual lunch than what good sense dictated. A handsome man like Reed Parker probably had more women in his life than she cared to count.

"Jackie?" Norm Timmons poked his head into her office, putting a halt to her wandering thoughts.

She looked up to see her boss's newly capped teeth glaring from his mouth like a child showing off his first permanent tooth. Beside him stood a tall attractive blond. "Yes, Norm?"

He motioned to the woman beside him. "I'd like you to meet Melanie Copeland, our new manager for the real estate loan department. Melanie, this is Jackie Mason."

Rising to her feet, Jackie peered up into ice blue eyes veiled in heavy lashes. With a sincere smile, she extended her hand. "Pleased to meet you, Melanie. I'm so glad you're here."

The lovely woman returned her gesture and grasped her hand. "I understand you've been under quite a workload. I'm so sorry. Norm tells me you are extremely capable, organized, and have been doing an excellent job."

"Thank you, but he's much too kind," Jackie replied, flashing a cordial glance at Norm before resuming eye contact with Melanie. "It will be so nice not to take papers home every evening and be able to live a real life."

"I don't blame you." Melanie's straight, shoulder-length, blond hair bounced as she spoke. "I'm involved in several meetings the rest of today, but tomorrow I'd like to begin working with you."

"Sounds great." Jackie thought the impeccable-looking woman before her seemed extremely pleasant.

"Do have patience with me. I want to learn everything thoroughly."

"Oh, we'll have plenty of time, and this will be fun."

Norm cleared his throat. "I can see you two won't run out of things to talk about. We must get going; Wilson is expecting us for a meeting."

Jackie nodded. "It's been a pleasure, Melanie. Tomorrow we'll get started, and you'll have the loan department shipshape in no time at all."

"I'm so excited about the position," she replied, leaning slightly over the desk.

"If you need anything at all, please feel free to stop by my office. Toledo is not a huge city, but I may be able to save you some footsteps," Jackie offered.

Melanie brightened. "Oh, I lived here eight years ago, so I'm fine."

Norm flashed Jackie a look and the two hastily said their good-byes. She watched them exit down the hall toward the elevators. Melanie wore an expensive, black silk suit with heels that would have destroyed Jackie's feet in an hour's time. More power to her! What a wonderful Monday. Lunch with Reed and a new manager for the real estate department all in one day.

five

"So now all I have to do is show the new manager our bank's routine, procedures, and what I've done. Then I'm back to working a regular day with—" Jackie stopped and cringed. "Here I am boring you to death, rattling on about bank business. I'm so sorry."

"You're not boring me." Reed glanced up from his menu and grinned. "I saw the papers and files on your desk. And remember? I couldn't get an appointment with you until Wednesday about my loan. Certainly glad I'm a patient man."

She eyed him suspiciously with a mischievous twinkle in her hazel eyes. "So that's why you invited me to lunch," she accused good-naturedly. "Hmm, want that house pretty bad, huh? Guess I'll put your application at the bottom of the pile."

He put down the menu and leaned back in his chair. "Can't believe you found me out already."

"Took me only a few days to put the pieces together. Didn't I tell you that I'm a private detective in my spare time?"

"You're clever. I don't suppose you'd reconsider."

"I might." She rested her cheek on her forefinger and thumb and set aside her menu. "What's your best offer?"

I like her more and more all the time, he thought, his mind racing with the ease of their bantering. "Give me a moment," he replied, shaking his head sadly. "Perhaps you've outsmarted me."

She giggled. "I doubt it. Remember, I looked over your loan application, and you have a very impressive position at General Motors, one that requires intelligence."

His eyes widened. "So, how about lunch on Wednesday, before our appointment?"

Shrugging her slender shoulders, Jackie tilted her head. She'd pulled back her hair and neatly tucked it at her nape.

Classy, he decided. He'd already admired her heather gray, pin-striped suit accented with a rose, gray, and cream scarf. . . definitely professional and feminine.

"I could consider lunch as bargaining power," she said, insinuating she carried the clout of a top executive.

"Okay, you're driving a hard deal here. Let me add another ploy. What about dinner on Friday. . .and a movie?"

"If we weren't teasing, I'd accept."

"Who's teasing? I'm serious." He looked with amazement.

She hesitated and gazed sincerely into his eyes. "I feel really uncomfortable about this, as though I've lured you into asking me out. I don't push myself on others—ever."

He smiled slowly. "Oh, you're not. This is all my contriving." He didn't need to deliberate. "Miss Mason, would you do me the honor of lunch on Wednesday and dinner on Friday, complete with a movie? How's that? And I don't expect any preferential treatment with my loan application."

"You're certain?" she asked with a slight frown on her lovely face.

"Absolutely."

She nibbled on her lower lip for a brief moment. "All right. Lunch and dinner it is."

"Great. Say, does this new loan officer mean I won't get your individual attention on my construction loan?"

She shook her head. "You still have me through closing, but she may need to follow up on a few things."

"I hope so," he said in a hushed tone, but before he could comment further, the waiter approached. "We'd better order soon, or you'll be working through our lunch on Wednesday."

She instantly focused on the menu, and for the first time in a long time, he didn't feel awkward in a woman's presence.

☙

Jackie found herself humming most of the afternoon. She sorted through papers and reduced a large stack of files down to the cherry wood finish on her desk. It had been months since she'd seen the top of her work area.

Odd, she couldn't remember what she ate for lunch. The

special? It didn't matter. She'd enjoyed a splendid hour with Reed Parker. He didn't seem so nervous today, but more relaxed. He actually appeared to enjoy himself.

Although being attracted to a man because of his appearance went against her personal convictions, he looked. . .well, simply gorgeous. He'd worn a cream-colored polo-type shirt and dark brown slacks. With his build, he could have worn patched overalls and still been the best-looking man at the restaurant. And his cologne. . .not overpowering, not too sweet or spicy, but a mixture of subtle woodsy scents that put him in a category by himself—a little mysterious and definitely intriguing.

In truth, she needed to know more about him, especially his spiritual beliefs. Today at lunch, she asked to give the blessing when he didn't offer. He agreed, but she should have questioned him. Yoking herself with an unbeliever went against everything she believed. A long time ago she'd made the mistake of falling in love with a man who had no use for God. She thought she could convert him; but after much heartache, she learned that only God can change a man's heart. Breaking off the relationship proved difficult, and she vowed then to never date a man who didn't love the Lord above all things.

He appears to be a good, gentle man, she told herself. *But goodness doesn't necessarily mean he's sold out to Jesus.* Tapping her nail on the desk, she chastised herself for failing to find out the answer to the most important question of all. *I'll just ask him on Wednesday,* she decided, but the lingering thought needled her.

Picking up the phone, she dialed her mother. After all, she knew Reed's parents and might be able to ease her mind about some things. It rang three times before her mother's cheerful voice answered.

"Hi, Mom."

"Hi, sweetie. What is it? I hear something wrong in your voice."

"Oh, Mom, I'm fine." She skirted the issue. "I just called to see what you were doing."

"Jackie," her mother reprimanded lightly, "you may be all grown-up, but I can still tell when you need to talk."

Jackie laughed. "All right, you win. I do have some good news, though."

"What's that?"

"The bank has hired a woman to take over the real estate department."

"Wonderful! And you've met her?"

Jackie smiled. "Yes, and she's very professional and personable. We start working together tomorrow. My first impression is we'll work well together."

"I'll be praying for both of you."

"Thanks, Mom." She took a deep breath.

"Out with it," her mother coaxed. "Do I need to come up there and set you down with a cup of coffee?"

Jackie giggled. "No, I suppose not, so here goes. Remember I asked you about Reed Parker?"

"Yes, and you saw him at the park with the kids on Saturday. By the way, they're still talking about him, or rather his dog."

Memories of the previous Saturday's encounter sent a tingle from Jackie's toes to her heart. "Well, we had lunch today."

"And?"

"He asked me for lunch on Wednesday and out to dinner on Friday. Without thinking, I accepted."

"So, what's the problem?"

Jackie swallowed hard. "I didn't ask him about his religious convictions, and I wondered if you could tell me anything."

"Honey, you need to talk to Reed about his relationship with the Lord. Now, his parents are good Christian people, and they are extremely proud of their son and what he's doing with his life. I will say his mother and I are rather close, and I think she would have shared with me if her son didn't know the Lord."

Jackie sighed with relief.

"But, honey," her mother cautioned, "she did say that some years back, he gave them a rough time. I don't know what happened, except he had problems."

"I understand," Jackie said thoughtfully. "You're right; I'll ask him about it on Wednesday."

"Good. So you like him?"

Again Jackie hesitated. "From what little time I've been with him, I guess I could say I like him."

"Another matter of prayer."

"Yes, definitely." Seeing one of her other phone lines light up, she regretted shortening the conversation. "Listen, Mom, someone is calling me. I've got to go."

"Okay. Call me later if you need to talk."

"I will, and I love you!"

"Love you, too."

Feeling much better, Jackie answered the other line.

"Jackie, this is Reed."

"Hi." She felt her pulse quicken at the sound of his voice.

"I don't want to take up too much of your time, but. . . well, I really enjoyed lunch today."

Pleased with his admission, she felt a warm blush creep up to her cheeks. "Thank you. I did, too."

"Well, I'll let you get back to work. Bye."

She replaced the receiver, feeling excited and energetic. Suddenly a cloud passed over her delicious musings and settled in the pit of her stomach. On Wednesday, she also had to tell him the truth about her past. Certainly nothing pleasant and she couldn't change a thing about it. It might be the last time she saw Reed Parker.

Pushing all those tumultuous thoughts from her head, she picked up a file and double-checked its contents for a closing in one hour.

≈

Slipping her feet from her heels beneath the desk, Melanie allowed her mind to drift back to when she'd previously lived in Toledo. What a nasty affair. Luckily, she'd learned from that game. Playing Reed along until three weeks before the wedding had been one of her favorite escapades, except her parents had exploded when they heard she'd broken the engagement. She'd enjoyed the charade of the "nice, sweet" girl who allowed the pressure of those around her to influence her marital decision. Frankly, she still found it rather humorous and certainly entertaining. She allowed her mother to return the wedding shower gifts, but she refused to give back the diamond. Instead, she had it remounted into a lovely dinner ring. Now, she rarely communicated with her parents. Such bores. They didn't understand the world's way of doing things at all. She'd been slated for money and power. Pity whoever got in her way.

Wonder what Reed's doing these days? she pondered. Tonight she'd search through the phone book and maybe give him a call. So what if a wife answered? Melanie didn't care. She laughed out loud, thinking about how sweetly she could say, "I'm an old friend, and I know he'd want to talk to me."

Of course Reed would want to see her, no matter how devoted his wife or how many kids he might have. He'd been a sentimental sort, and she possessed a mind that never forgot a word or display of emotion. She had a way with him, like she did with all men. Tell them what they want to hear, or let them think they can have what they want, and men were marshmallows.

Already, Norm Timmons indicated his interest. Disgusting little fat man with his hedgehog hairpiece, but he was her boss. She could concede to a few grabbling moments for position's sake. Wilson Anderson, on the other hand, had a powerful flair about him. After their initial meeting this morning, she knew he liked her. Sandy-blond hair, deep blue, almost purple eyes, and a trim build. Not bad for a forty-something man who had a rising future with Today's Bank. She remembered seeing a picture on his desk of his wife and four kids. At the time, she commented on his handsome family. But they didn't matter if she set her sights on him; the family only upped how much he'd be willing to pay her when she grew tired of him. Yes, moving back to Toledo might be fun.

Then again, Reed might be a source of amusement for awhile until someone better came along.

six

"Jackie, you really are organized," Melanie said, as Jackie explained her filing system. "Your system will certainly simplify my job."

"I hope so. The easier the transition, the less frustrating it will be for you. I know you have your own way of doing things, but I've downloaded my procedures, and the hard copy is in a file with your name on it." Jackie leaned over the desk and pointed. "There it is on the right-hand corner. You won't hurt my feelings one bit if you toss it into the trash."

Melanie's ice blue eyes widened at the file's contents. "This is such a tremendous help. No wonder Wilson speaks highly of you. You're going to be a tough act to follow."

Jackie laughed. "I doubt that. From what Norm's told me, you will have this department humming along in no time at all. I do want to help you with the customers who haven't closed on their loans yet, but you can take over any new business as soon as you feel you're ready."

"Sounds fair to me. May I see the pending files?"

"Of course. They're on the left-hand corner of the credenza behind you. One client has requested I personally complete his loan, and his information is on my desk."

Melanie nodded and began leafing through the stack of applications. Jackie noted how stunning Melanie appeared in her red fitted suit, although the skirt seemed a little short. Maybe women dressed differently in Chicago. An instant later, Jackie's rumbling stomach caused her to take a quick glance at her watch. "It's nearly noon, Melanie. Would you like to go to lunch?"

"Sure. Yesterday I went with Norm." Her voice lowered. "Don't want to do that again for awhile."

Jackie chose not to comment. No point in gossiping, and

41

she felt certain Melanie could handle the man. "Tell you what, I need to take some paperwork up to Wilson's office, and then we can leave. Okay?"

"Perfect, it will give me time to sort through these files. How long will you be gone?"

"Probably fifteen minutes."

Melanie smiled. "I'll be right here."

As Jackie walked toward the stairs leading to Wilson's office, she thanked God for blessing her with such a sweet coworker. Now the stress would lighten, and the weight of her position seemed to lift from her shoulders. She felt a twinge of guilt in not asking Melanie to lunch yesterday. It would have spared her from Norm and his inappropriate advances.

"Hi, Carla," she greeted, flashing a smile at Wilson's secretary. "How are you?"

"Just about perfect," the matronly, silver-headed woman replied. "I bet you're excited about Miss Copeland filling the real estate position."

"Absolutely. She's extremely pleasant and quite capable. I think it will work out wonderfully." Jackie glanced at the office behind Carla. "Is Wilson available?"

"No. He took an early lunch with his wife. Can I give him a message?" She reached for a pink message pad and snatched up a pen.

"You can tell him the morning went well with Melanie Copeland, and here are the files for this afternoon's closings. I'll be handling those at two and three-thirty. Most likely I will have Melanie sit in with me."

Carla jotted down the information. "All right. I've got it."

"Thanks." Jackie headed back downstairs. As she neared her office, she saw Melanie quickly close a file and set it down on Jackie's desk. Then she turned and began leafing through some other files. Confused, Jackie stopped and observed her further. Why did Melanie look so. . .secretive?

❧

Reed munched on a bag of chips at his desk, then washed down the remains with a bottle of water. Eating in his office didn't have the same atmosphere of Jackie's company or her pretty face, but if he closed his eyes and concentrated he could hear the ring of her voice. To be perfectly honest with himself, he'd fallen hard and in less than a week. Jackie had taken control of his emotions and revived those feelings he thought had died. Reed wanted to call her, but he'd seen her yesterday and would again tomorrow. Still, the thought tempted him.

He crumpled up the empty chip bag and tossed it into the trash. Now, just where could he take Jackie to lunch—or for that matter, dinner on Friday? Swinging his chair around to the computer screen, he decided to run a search on the latest movies, their ratings, and reviews.

"Working your lunch hour?" Nathan asked.

Reed whirled around to find his friend leaning into the doorway. "No, just doing some personal research."

"How's the house deal?"

Reed grinned. "Going great. If all goes well, the construction should get under way in about four weeks."

"You know Kathi is fit to be tied with you building a home of your own." Nathan ran his fingers over his balding head. "In fact, we drove around looking at new constructions on Sunday. I can't complain; we are long overdue for a place of our own."

"Exactly how I felt."

"Say, we're wondering if you wanted to come by Friday for dinner?"

Reed's agenda floated across his mind. "I'm sorry, but I've already made plans."

Nathan raised a brow and smiled broadly. "Couldn't be Jackie, now could it?"

"Perhaps."

"That's what I thought. Well, if you have time, bring her by. Kathi is anxious to meet her."

"Um, sounds good to me. We're heading to dinner and a movie, but there might be time between the two."

Nathan shook his head. "Don't worry about it. We can get

together at another time."

"I'd like for us to get together," Reed replied. "Jackie's a special lady."

Nathan grinned. "Has to be to put up with you. See ya later."

Reed waved and spun around to his computer. He connected to the Internet and typed the site for movies. Unable to stand not hearing her voice a moment longer, he picked up the phone and dialed the bank's number. Once the operator transferred the call to the real estate loan department, he waited patiently on the line.

A strangely familiar voice answered the phone. Reed frowned, knowing he'd dialed Jackie's direct extention. "Is Jackie Mason available?"

"Not right at the moment. May I take a message?" a female politely asked.

"Sure. Would you tell her Reed Parker called?"

"Of course. Does she have your number?"

"Yes."

"I'll tell her you phoned."

Reed replaced the receiver. Why did that woman's voice sound so familiar?

Hours later, he switched off the light in his office and headed for the parking lot. Jackie hadn't returned his call. Perhaps she'd been too busy with her heavy workload and training the new loan officer.

❧

Wednesday, shortly before noon, Jackie slipped back into her chair after carefully assessing herself in the ladies' room. Makeup reapplied, hair pulled back from her face and neatly brushed down her back, the usual butterflies taking flight in her stomach, all added up to one thing: Soon she'd be in the company of Reed Parker. In an amazingly short time, she'd found herself spending every spare minute thinking about him—how he carried himself. . .his slow easy smile. . .and those incredible long dark lashes.

But today she intended to take care of a few pressing matters. He probably had guessed she was a Christian, but she needed to confirm it and ask about his stand with the Lord. Reed could easily capture a corner of her heart; in fact, he already tugged at it. But she couldn't allow their relationship to blossom any further if he hadn't given his life to the Lord.

The second matter, however, took a little more courage. It centered around her nationality. Reed deserved to know the truth about her race, no matter what the outcome. It wouldn't be the first time an intriguing man lost interest because she explained her adoption.

"Heading for lunch?" Melanie asked, stopping outside Jackie's office.

"Yes, shortly," Jackie replied, suddenly feeling uncomfortable about leaving Melanie alone, especially if Norm pestered her. "I'm meeting a friend here."

"Well, I plan to bring in a salad and look over some closings, if you don't mind." She picked up a lock of blond hair and tossed it over her shoulder.

"I feel like I'm deserting you."

Melanie shook her head. "Goodness, don't be concerned about me. Norm invited me to lunch this morning, so I had to come up with something fast." When Jackie failed to reply, she continued. "Anyway, I really need to study your client files, and this provides the perfect opportunity."

"All right, but take some time for yourself, and be sure to shut the door to your office or you won't have any privacy." Jackie smiled. "I don't want you burned out before you even get started."

Melanie laughed. "No danger of that. I assure you I can work around the clock."

Jackie glanced behind Melanie and saw Reed waiting outside her office. "Oh, my friend is here," she said. "Would you like to meet him?"

"Sure," Melanie replied as Jackie stood from her desk. "I'll follow you."

Jackie felt herself grow warm as she returned Reed's smile. "Hi," she softly greeted. "You look great."

Immediately, the color faded from his face and a look of

surprise and coldness met her gaze. *What happened?* she wondered.

"Reed," Melanie cooed, rushing past Jackie and throwing her arms around his neck. "It has been so long. How are you?" She giggled excitedly. "I shouldn't have asked—I can see you are as devilishly handsome as ever." In stretching to embrace his neck, her short mint green skirt inched up the back of her legs. In an instant, she pressed a wine-colored kiss against his lips.

Jackie glanced away, embarrassed. Reed hadn't even kissed her, but she'd certainly thought about it.

Reed stood stoically, then gently pushed Melanie to arms' length. Not giving him a moment to speak, she reached up to hug him again.

"So this is who you are having lunch with?" Melanie asked, glancing accusingly at Jackie. "He is the best. I could tell you stories. . ."

"That's not necessary," Reed interrupted. His jaw tightened and he sighed heavily. He peered over the top of Melanie's head to Jackie. She wasn't sure what to say or do.

"Are you ready, Jackie?" he asked firmly. His voice sounded strained.

She nodded, slightly bewildered—and a little jealous at the familiarity her coworker was demonstrating with her Reed. *My Reed! What am I thinking?* "Yes, of course," she replied, more calmly than she actually felt.

"Oh, let me come, too," Melanie squealed, glancing from Reed to Jackie and back again. "We've got so much catching up to do." Her ice blue eyes turned to Jackie. "It's been eight long years since I've seen this man."

Jackie swallowed hard. "It's up to Reed."

"I don't think so," he instantly replied. "It's not a good idea."

Melanie played with a button on his maroon pullover. "Please," she whined. "We have so much catching up to do. I want to hear how you two met and how long you've been seeing each other."

He pushed her hand away. "No."

Jackie ached for Melanie. Reed sounded angry, a side of him not evident before. *Why is he so upset? What's going on here?*

"How are your parents?" Melanie asked gently. "Does your father still collect old locomotive trains?"

Reed said nothing.

"I guess I owe you an apology," she said, taking a step backward. "I've changed, Reed, really I have." She hesitated and wrung her hands. Long, empty moments passed while she peered at the floor. Finally she lifted watery eyes to his face. Jackie saw the tears, and her heart went out to the distraught woman. "Will you give me a chance, please?" Melanie pleaded. "I. . .I'm a Christian now."

seven

"And do you remember the time we took the ferry to Catawba Island and bicycled in the rain? Our picnic got soaked and somehow you lost your wallet. And then we were stranded there with no food or money until your dad came. I'll never forget the disgusted look he gave us when we met him at the ferry."

Reed successfully feigned indifference to Melanie's reminiscing. Jackie didn't need to hear about what happened nearly nine years ago. He had lived those days in another lifetime. Back then he worshiped the ground around Melanie, and he spent every waking moment trying to please her. Much later he discovered his futile efforts.

Truthfully, the words spilling from her mouth brought back a flood of unwanted memories. He wanted to shout at her to stop, but he feared she'd smile smugly and silently claim that he hadn't gotten over her.

But he had mended his heart through the prayers and assistance of wonderful friends and family who refused to give up on him. Now, he could get through this detestable hour with Melanie. She'd destroyed him before but never again. With his eyes focused on her flawless face, Reed braced himself and relied completely upon God.

Stealing a glance at Jackie, who sat stiffly with a pasted smile on her face, he felt a new surge of anger. She hadn't touched a bite of her food. For that matter, neither had he, and this restaurant prepared the best seafood in the city. His gaze captured her hazel eyes and a faint glimmer of longing passed between them. They hadn't been able to exchange two words without Melanie monopolizing the conversation. *Of course*, he thought regretfully, *she always had to be the center of attention.*

At that moment, he would have given a week's salary to have Melanie anywhere than here in the same restaurant.

At least he'd have Jackie to himself on Friday, if she'd still go out with him. Strangely enough, he wanted to explain Melanie and their disastrous relationship. Well, not all of it, but certainly some of the truth. He'd grown to care for Jackie in such a short while, and in time, he would tell her the whole story.

He lifted the water glass to his lips.

"Do you still drink gallons of water?" Melanie questioned with a flirtatious glint in her ice blue eyes. "And I know just when you need your thirst quenched."

He maintained control, but inside he bit back a string of unkind remarks. She hadn't changed a bit, and her implications made his blood boil. Hopefully Jackie didn't understand all of the nasty barbs and quips thrown his way.

And Melanie claimed to be a believer. *Let's see how you fake your way through this,* he inwardly challenged, fighting the urge to leave her sitting alone while he escorted Jackie to another restaurant.

"So, tell me, how did you become a Christian?" he asked. As soon as the words left his mouth, he felt a twinge of remorse. He had no right to judge her. His walk with God hadn't won any blue ribbons either, yet he did feel responsible to discern her actions. He sensed she was playing a game of cat and mouse.

"Yes, of course," Melanie replied. "While living in Chicago, a friend habitually invited me to church each week until I finally consented. I sensed I'd have no peace until I accompanied him. Anyway, I dreaded the whole thing—missing my sleep on Sunday morning and having to dress up just like a regular day. Well, the choir impressed me with the quality of their music, but the minister's words pierced my heart. At the close of the sermon, he asked if anyone wanted to receive Christ into their life to walk down front to the altar, so I stepped out of the pew and did that very thing."

"How long has it been?" Reed questioned, taking another sip of water.

She tilted her blond head thoughtfully. "I guess three years now."

Maybe she has turned her life around, he mused. *She's saying all of the right things. Lord, if she's turned her life over to You, please show me.*

"I guess I need your forgiveness for all the horrible things I said and did to you," she continued. Wide-eyed, she peered into his face. When he failed to reply, her voice quivered. "Reed, will you forgive me?"

Melanie sounded near tears, a ploy she'd used plenty of times when they were together. Back then, he gave into her every whim and desire, but now she wanted forgiveness for those dark-stained days. One look at her angelic face and those pale blue eyes convinced him she must be telling the truth.

"I forgive you," he repeated, pulling himself away from her gaze.

"Thank you. It means so much to me. I never dreamed I'd have the opportunity to share with you what the Lord has done in my life." Glancing at Jackie, she smiled charmingly. "I wish you two the best, and I apologize for intruding upon your lunch together. It seemed like a divine appointment to make amends for the horrible things I'd done and said."

"I enjoyed having you with us," Jackie said, "and I'll pray for you—in your walk with the Lord and your new position at the bank."

"What a dear, new friend you are." Melanie reached across the table and gently patted Jackie's arm. "Reed is so lucky to have you in his life." She turned to him. "All I want is for you and I to be friends."

With mounting apprehension, Reed listened and watched the scene unfold before him. Perhaps he'd been wrong about Melanie, but some of her old habits still grated on his nerves. Had she really changed? And why did he have these doubts when he should feel glad for her? God used all kinds of people to carry out His purpose, but something about Melanie didn't quite convince him of her conversion.

Reed cringed. He didn't have the answers, but he knew who did.

&

"Thanks for lunch," Jackie said, once Melanie had exited the Blazer. She felt awkward, not sure exactly what had transpired at lunch but certain she should not have accompanied Melanie and Reed.

He looked perplexed, and his brown eyes held a faraway look. The shyness from their beginning conversations now resurfaced.

"I'm really sorry about what happened at lunch," he said sincerely.

"It's all right, but I should be the one to apologize. You and Melanie could have spoken much more freely if I'd stayed at the bank."

"I wouldn't have gone anywhere without you," he instantly replied. "The time was to be with you. . .no one else."

Jackie smiled. "But Melanie needed to talk. She is very sweet, and I'm sure you value her friendship."

"Well. . .I suppose," he said slowly, massaging the back of his neck. "I'd like to talk to you about her. . .and our old relationship."

"All right," she replied, realizing the topic must be sensitive from his vagueness and unusual behavior during the noon hour. The problem was she hadn't spent enough time with Reed to really know him and predict his response to things. For that matter, she and Melanie were barely acquainted. Confused, she wondered if she should have guarded her feelings more closely with Reed.

"Do we still have a dinner date?"

She hesitated, concerned that he felt obligated. "Yes, if you are still interested."

"Definitely." He looked hurt, but then an easy smile spread across his handsome features. "I've looked forward to our date all week. Do you mind giving me your home phone number? I'd like to call later."

She jotted down her personal information on the back of her

business card and handed it to him. "I really need to get back to work, but I'll be home later tonight. Could we talk then?"

"Sure." He reached out and gently touched her shoulder, surprising her. "Jackie, be careful where Melanie is concerned. I know she says she's a believer, but I. . . Just be wary of her."

She chewed on her lower lip. She felt his situation with Melanie cut deeper than she initially perceived. "I will, but I don't understand."

"I know, and Friday night. . ." He sighed, a troubled look spread over his face. "Well, we may need to discuss it." Reed toyed with the lapel on her jacket. "I am looking forward to getting to know you better."

"Me, too." She exited the Blazer and turned once to wave good-bye.

Peering up at the bank, reality blew a cold chill around her. What had actually happened at lunch? Too many unspoken words and the looks Melanie and Reed exchanged led Jackie to believe they had been more than casual friends. But what? They appeared nothing alike, or were they?

❧

Melanie muffled a chuckle as Jackie walked by her office. Earlier this morning, she'd convinced Norm to let her work from her own office instead of Jackie's. She didn't need someone looking over her shoulder while she learned the particulars of this branch of Today's Bank. She had already grasped their procedures enough to take over her assigned department. Besides, she could take only so much of Miss Goody-goody.

Powerless to conceal her mirth, she stood and faced the window overlooking the building's parking lot and laughed. *Hmm.* She curled a strand of hair around her finger. *Reed Parker. . .what a charming twist this transfer to Toledo had taken. And to think he's seeing Jackie.* Melanie didn't know which bit of information proved more hilarious—having Reed nearby to amuse her or to discover he and Jackie were dating.

What fun! Melanie had been in a state of elation since she

had seen his folder on Jackie's desk. She knew the moment he called she didn't intend to give Jackie his message. It would have spoiled everything. She could simply imagine poor Reed's state of mind when Jackie didn't return his call. In years gone by, when Melanie refused to call or see him, it had driven him nearly insane. She liked possessing that kind of power over him—over all men who fell under her prey.

Today Jackie and Reed swallowed her Christian story. She felt sure of it. Good thing she'd asked Norm for Jackie and Wilson's background. It gave her time to educate herself on Christian jargon. Originally she planned to use the information to wiggle herself into Wilson's life and skirt around Jackie's prudish views, but now she saw another purpose. Reed.

Melanie remembered the days when he struggled with his religious beliefs and her incessant demands. She'd always won—and would again. Miss Jackie ought to do herself a favor and kiss him good-bye. Once Melanie tired of him again, Jackie wouldn't want him back. He'd be pathetic mush, but men like him deserved to be used. Maybe someday they'd learn you don't get a thing in this world unless you take it. And Melanie prided herself in taking everything her heart desired.

This afternoon she'd begin the game.

Melanie closed a file and headed to Jackie's office. "Hi," she greeted a few moments later. "Thanks again for allowing me to have lunch with you and Reed. I appreciated the opportunity to see him again and share my story."

Jackie locked her purse inside a drawer and nodded pleasantly. "You're more than welcome. I gather you two go back a long way."

"As a matter of fact, we do. At one time we were quite close." Melanie lifted a finger to her lips. "It's been over eight years now." She sighed and shook her head. Reaching for a tissue on Jackie's desk, she dabbed her eyes. "How long have you been dating?"

"We met recently, right here in this office."

"I see. He seems to have matured, and I'm thrilled for you."

Jackie lifted a brow, obviously questioning Melanie's deliberate attempt to dissuade her from a relationship with Reed.

"Oh, don't pay any attention to me. I didn't exactly live the proper life back then either." Her attention flitted about the room while she nervously wrung her hands. Finally she lifted another tissue to her eyes. "Well, we've both got work to do. I'll head back to my office."

eight

Reed sat at his kitchen table with his fingers wrapped around a steaming mug of coffee. He stared directly ahead—looking at nothing in particular, only remembering. The earlier encounter with Melanie had affected him more than he cared to admit. Flashbacks of the times they'd spent together haunted him. His whole world had centered around her beauty and charms, consuming him until he nearly choked to death. Willingly, he'd allowed her to pull him into an addictive affair that defiled everything he ever believed. It took years to put Melanie behind him and finally find his way back to God. He'd hoped never to see her again. A sick feeling rose and fell in his stomach.

He despised the things he'd done during those turbulent years. Love for Melanie had caused him to abandon his faith, his family, and his friends. No excuse. He couldn't blame anyone but himself. Only the knowledge of God's unconditional love had set him free from the painful memories.

Yukon nuzzled his leg. "Hey, fella," he said gently, patting his dog's head. "You know, I've finally found a great lady, and Melanie shows up. I wonder why? God does things for a reason, but this one baffles me. Melanie says she's changed, but a Christian wouldn't say some of things I heard this afternoon. I'm afraid for Jackie. Melanie never used to make friends with anyone unless she could use them." Yukon tilted his big head as if understanding Reed's words. "Melanie could easily chew her up before Jackie would realize what happened. Then again, perhaps I'm not giving Jackie enough credit; she may be stronger than I think. After all, Christians must be tough to take a stand for truth. But I don't trust Melanie. No, I don't trust her at all."

❧

Jackie's stomach churned. Reed said he'd pick her up at seven-thirty—in less than ten minutes, and she still wondered if she should go. Oh, she adored his company, and her emotions skyrocketed whenever she thought about him; but doubts about his character had plagued her since Wednesday afternoon. She recalled Melanie's enthusiasm at seeing Reed, but his apathy to Melanie's heartrending apology bothered Jackie. And what about his words of warning about Melanie? And later her new friend's tears and the statement about Reed's maturity? Who did she dare believe? If she trusted Reed, it put a damper on her recent friendship with Melanie and their working relationship. Casting aside Reed because she didn't understand his reactions didn't make sense either.

Oh, God, You are in control. Jackie faced her bathroom mirror and tugged on a stubborn curl. *You know what is best for all of us. I surrender my doubts to You about Reed, and I pray for wisdom in discerning the truth. Help me to see Your guiding hand.*

The doorbell rang. *Maybe I should have met him at the restaurant rather than allow him to pick me up. Too late now. What happened to my levelheaded cautious self?*

Once assured that Reed stood outside the door, she opened it. As usual, he looked like he had just stepped off the cover of a fashion magazine. *Be careful,* she warned herself. *Don't judge a man by his looks. Tonight, listen to his heart.*

❧

"This place is fabulous," Jackie whispered, after the starched waiter disappeared with their order. "Do you come here often?"

He raised a dark brow and chuckled. "No, hardly ever. Only once when a friend of mine brought his wife here for dinner, and I tagged along."

She smiled. "Well, I'm impressed." The exquisite restaurant with its amber lighting and the faint melodious sounds of a string quartet playing in the background slowly soothed her misgivings about the evening. She adored Reed's impeccable manners and deep voice. Shy and reserved, attentive and caring, he reminded her of a hero from a Victorian novel.

Now, before they ate, she needed to ask him about the Lord, and depending on his response, tell him about her race.

"Jackie?" he asked quietly.

Her gaze lifted to meet his, but in the dim light she couldn't see his eyes. She only heard the soft seriousness of his voice. "Yes?"

He leaned forward. "I've been doing a lot of thinking since Wednesday afternoon." He inhaled deeply. "I'd like to tell you about Melanie and me."

She attempted a faint smile. "I've been wondering myself, although I didn't feel I should ask."

"Has she told you anything about us?" A look of concern etched across his forehead.

"She said that over eight years ago, you two were close."

He nodded slowly and took a deep breath before beginning. "At one time, Melanie and I were engaged to be married. She broke it off three weeks before the wedding." He paused. "Honestly, Jackie, I don't know how much or how little to say about this."

Silence clamored around them, as she considered her response. "I guess whatever you feel is appropriate," she finally replied.

"Well, I think you should hear the reason why she cancelled the wedding," he said. "First off, let me state that Melanie and I went through weeks of premarital counseling with a strong emphasis on the obvious problems facing us due to the racial differences. I thought we had worked through all the issues because she never indicated any doubts. But I was mistaken. Three weeks prior to our wedding, she gave me a good-bye letter and left for Chicago. I hadn't seen or heard from her until yesterday."

"I'm sorry," Jackie whispered. "How very hard for you."

"It caused a few sleepless nights." Reed gave her a half smile. "But there's more, and this is what I hesitate to tell you. If it hadn't been for good friends and family who loved the Lord and me, I would have ended up pushing myself into an early grave. Up until the breakup, I thought being a Christian meant just going to church. Oh, I knew the talk and I'd heard the gospel, but I never took any of it seriously. So with my heart broken, I spent my time in drunkenness, wild parties, bad company, and the like. I stooped to some pretty degrading things before God allowed me to nearly kill myself in a motorcycle accident. That jarred my senses and I surrendered my life to Jesus Christ." Reed stared long into her eyes. "I know you are a very godly woman, and I understand if my past is not what you desire."

Jackie swallowed the lump forming in her throat. She believed him, and nothing he'd said discouraged her from continuing their relationship. "What I care about is your relationship with God today."

"I don't think I'll ever be content with what I do for Him. I am a Christian, and as the cliché goes, I'm sold out to Jesus."

"I couldn't ask for more." She sensed his passion to be more like Christ.

He grasped his glass of water and swirled the ice. Glancing up, she caught his gaze and he sighed. "I hope Melanie has found the Lord, but I admit that I—well, time will answer my questions."

Jackie's sigh echoed his. "Now I understand your reaction toward her, and I'm not so sure I could have been so gracious. It must have been horrible to see Melanie and relive the hurt she'd caused."

"Well, let's say, I've been in more pleasant circumstances— like spending the evening with you."

She felt herself grow warm. "Well, thank you for telling me. I really appreciate your honesty, and I don't feel any differently about you, except I admire your strength during lunch Wednesday." She lifted her hands to the table. "I have something to tell you, too."

"Is this our evening of honesty?" he asked softly.

"Yes, maybe so. And I'll understand if you don't want to pursue any further dates."

His brown eyes softened. "Jackie, I can't imagine anything you could tell me that would stop me from wanting to see you."

She glanced down at her folded hands and felt her heart pound. How many times had she been through this and heard those same words before? "Reed, you already know I'm adopted." When he nodded, she continued. "What you don't know is that no one can tell me about my parents. I was abandoned as an infant with no traces of my heritage. In other words, I can't give you any racial information about myself."

He didn't hesitate to respond. "I don't care if you are from Mars or turn neon orange and green at midnight." He reached across the table and took her hand. "I haven't dated since Melanie broke our engagement. Attempting any kind of a relationship with a woman is extremely difficult for me, as I'm sure you are aware." He smiled. "The first time I met you, I saw a beautiful lady—inside and out. You, as a person, are important to me. There's more to Jackie Mason than color or race. I care about your heart."

Relief washed over her as she fought the urge to weep. Not only did Reed serve the Lord, but he also accepted the ambiguity of her heritage. This man, this wonderful man of whom she'd grown very fond in such a short time, had just paid her the highest compliment imaginable.

"You're rather quiet," he remarked softly.

She smiled. "I'm happy."

He shook his head, and she noticed he still held her hand. "Impossible—happy is what you make me."

"It works both ways."

He cradled her hand and squeezed it gently. "That's the best news yet."

Jackie blinked back the wetness threatening to spill down her cheeks. Being with Reed felt perfect. How she hoped God intended this man for her. At that moment, she wanted to believe nothing could ever stand in the way of their growing relationship.

Not color.

Not race.

Not even memories of Melanie.

★

Reed whipped off his tie and draped it around the doorknob of his closet. What a great evening. Being with Jackie brought out the very best in him. He felt like singing, but the neighbors on the other side of the walls might not value his off-key bass. For that matter, Yukon might object.

He chuckled. Could this be love? Did he dare turn handsprings and celebrate? It felt great to have Jackie return his affections without her making selfish demands. He'd seen a spark of love in her hazel eyes—and he didn't intend to let it go out!

They'd made plans for tomorrow afternoon to take in a baseball game. He didn't care what they did, as long as they were together.

Thanks, Lord. I know to be cautious and take this slow, but this seems so perfect.

The phone rang, interrupting his racing thoughts. "Hello?"

"Hi, Reed." He stiffened at the sultry sound of Melanie's voice on the line. For a moment, he felt tempted to hang up. "Am I interrupting anything?"

His throat tightened. "As a matter of fact, you are."

"Oh? Is Jackie there?"

The insinuation irritated him. "No, I'm just tired and want to go to bed."

"Poor man; you work too hard." Her voice rang dangerously seductive.

"Melanie, what do you want?"

She giggled. "Just to hear your voice and talk."

"Well, now you've talked to me, so you can go on about your business."

"Right now, you are my business."

Agitation plodded across his emotions. "I don't think so."

"But I've missed you."

He despised her whining. "Sorry, I'm wonderful without you."

"You don't mean that. We had great times."

"Yeah, well, the past is dead and I have no intentions of conjuring it up."

"Now, you've hurt my feelings, and I'm doing my best to show you I've changed."

"I'm glad you've turned your life around." He felt his temper escalate with each word pouring from her mouth.

"Can't we get together. . .like we used to?" she asked barely above a whisper.

"No. Simply not interested. Look, I'm tired. Good night." He replaced the phone and pounded his fist into the palm of his hand.

The phone rang again, but he refused to pick it up. Instead the answering machine took the message.

"Reed, I don't like it when someone hangs up on me, especially when it's someone I care about. We will get back together. You wait and see. I don't ever give up on things I want." *Click.*

Reed swallowed, his throat dry. The threatening implication in Melanie's voice sent chills up his spine. He well remembered all the devious ways she used to seize what she wanted. Melanie could be dangerous, and this pretense of Christianity—for he felt certain it was exactly that—wouldn't work with him. He had the Commander in Chief on his side.

nine

Exiting her car on Monday morning, Jackie felt like she'd been riding first-class on a magic carpet since Friday night—without holding on. Her feet hadn't touched ground, and her mind danced after all those special moments with Reed.

What a wonderful weekend they'd shared! She'd even found a new admiration for baseball, especially when the Toledo Mud Hens won on Saturday afternoon. Jackie and Reed's moments together were simply exquisite.

Sharing a foot-long chili hotdog loaded with onions.

Caramel corn and peanuts.

An evening spring rain that left her ponytail in long ringlets.

His baseball jacket that silenced her chattering teeth.

Sunday afternoon with Yukon at the park, playing Frisbee. And a long, long walk with them holding hands and laughing about everything. Then. . .

"Thanks for a great weekend," Reed had said Sunday night at her apartment door. His fingers entwined with hers, holding on tightly. She hated to say good night and sensed he didn't want their time together to end either.

"I had a wonderful time." She leaned against her door.

He brushed a wayward curl from her cheek. "There's only one thing I would have changed."

"What's that?" Jackie asked.

"We should have gone to church together."

"An excellent suggestion."

"How about next Sunday?" Reed whispered, inching closer to her face. Thick eyelashes veiled the tenderness in his brown eyes.

"Yours or mine?"

"Both." He smiled. "Of course, my parents will talk."

Jackie laughed lightly. "Mine, too."

"I don't care," Reed declared firmly.

"Me, either."

"Jackie, I have a question."

"Ask away."

"May I kiss you?"

Her stomach flipped. "Please do."

It was a light brush against her lips. He didn't hold her tightly or intensify the moment.

Later, while trying to sleep, she remembered the kiss. Reed. . .such a gentleman. Without saying anything, she knew he understood the dangers of physical contact between a man and a woman. Especially those attracted to each other. Yes, Jackie could get used to him very easily.

❧

The next morning, climbing the steps to the bank building, Jackie caught sight of Wilson and waved.

"Good morning, Jackie," he called. "Wasn't the choir at church good yesterday?"

"Excellent," she agreed. "Your children certainly are growing up fast."

Wilson grinned. "Yeah, probably too fast. Becky says she can't keep them in shoes and peanut butter." He held the door for her. "Glad to hear Miss Copeland is working out well."

Jackie nodded, suddenly remembering the things Reed had revealed about Melanie. "Oh, yes," she hastily said, "from the way she caught on to our procedures, it won't be long before she'll be handling the real estate department by herself."

He smiled, and she saw the approval in his deep blue eyes. "Glad to hear it." The vice president headed upstairs to his office.

After greeting the receptionist, Jackie turned down the hallway to her office. She didn't know if she wanted to see Melanie or not. Granted, they'd started as friends, but that was before lunch on Wednesday. Oh, well, if she could work with Norm Timmons, she could work with anyone.

Greeting coworkers as she walked, Jackie hurried down

the hall to her office. She seldom minded Mondays; in fact, she rather enjoyed planning a new week. And this morning, she wouldn't need two cups of coffee to wake her up. Thanks to Reed Parker, she still soared above the clouds.

A crystal vase of deep red roses on her desk caught her eye. *Who could have sent these so early in the morning?* she mused.

Stepping closer, Jackie saw an envelope resting beneath the vase. Curious, she slid it from the glass container and opened it to an ivory sheet of stationery.

> *Jackie,*
>
>   *Thank you so much for helping me during my first week. I couldn't have made it without you. More importantly, thank you for being my friend. Your thoughtful ways calmed my frenzied nerves and made me feel welcome. Surely you are an angel sent from heaven to make this transition easier for me.*
>
>   *I am so sorry for creating such a scene with Reed last Wednesday. I don't know what came over me. I guess seeing him after all these years brought back precious memories. Please forgive me, and I do wish you the best with him. You deserve excellence.*
>
>   *Melanie*

Jackie bent to inhale the sweet fragrance of the roses. Bewildered by Melanie's gesture of friendship and Reed's explanation of their past relationship, she suddenly felt terribly confused. Could Reed be wrong about her?

Dear God, what is going on here? I'm so mixed up, and I don't understand any of this. Could Reed be wrong? Has Melanie really changed?

                        ஐ

From the doorway of her office, Melanie observed Jackie reading the note she'd left with the flowers, then saw her glance off in obvious contemplation. Melanie wished she could see the expression on Jackie's face. *The twit probably hoped they were from Reed,* she thought with an inward sneer. *I have already received more roses from him than she ever will.*

Melanie slipped back into her office before Jackie detected her. Snatching up a file, she eased down into her chair and began leafing through it. She stole a quick peek at her desk clock and wondered how long until Jackie graced her office. Five minutes? Two minutes?

Thirty seconds later, Melanie heard a light rap on her door. Dressed in a celery green linen jacket and long skirt, Jackie wore a gracious smile and held the note in her hand. She reminded Melanie of a faded asparagus. At least the silver accessories were in proportion to her outfit. Miss Goody-goody's only attractive features were her long, thick curly hair and huge hazel eyes. Still, if she expected to hook Reed, she needed to shorten those skirts and lower the neckline.

"The flowers are beautiful," Jackie said, stepping inside the office. She lightly waved the note. "And I'm so glad to have assisted you last week. You were a delight to train—and the flowers weren't necessary at all. But thanks for your thoughtfulness and kind words."

"You're quite welcome; just enjoy them."

"Where did you find roses so early in the morning?" Jackie asked.

Melanie tilted her head and offered a smile. "I found a place nearby that opens very early—kind of a doughnut, coffee, and get-your-flowers-here spot. In fact, I saw Norm there around six-thirty this morning."

Jackie looked aghast. "You got up that early for me? How sweet!"

"Well, you are such a dear person, and I wanted to repay you in some way for your hard work. You know, I meant every word in your note, especially where Reed is concerned. I will never make a pest of myself again."

"You weren't a pest."

Melanie forced a shiver of remorse and massaged her arms. "Oh, yes, I was. I'm ashamed of myself for pushing him to reminisce about those years we spent together. My actions didn't show much for my Christianity. Am I forgiven?"

"Oh, of course. Don't worry another minute about it."

"Good," Melanie replied, contriving a sincere smile. "Again you've shown me what a wonderful friend you truly are."

"I simply care about you," Jackie said. She rubbed her hands together and laughed. "With all these compliments, I'd better get back to work before your praises go to my head." She turned to leave, then whirled around. "If you need anything, please let me know."

"I will, and do you mind if I use your office during lunch today? I'm trying to finish up this paperwork, and some of the files are still in your cabinet."

"Be my guest!"

Through the glass door, Melanie watched Jackie disappear down the hall. What a pushover! Jackie's gullibility almost spoiled the fun. No wonder she swallowed that Christian babble; only a fool would believe such junk. From all the visible evidence, Melanie had inched closer to fooling Jackie.

Tapping her recently manicured nails on the desktop, Melanie oozed with satisfaction. Getting up early to find the flower shop seemed worth the effort. Luckily it was close to the bank, but then she'd run into Norm there. He'd persuaded her to sit through his three doughnuts and listen to his come-on clichés before driving to work. Still, with a little sweetness on her part, Melanie could coax any information she wanted from him.

As though on cue, she saw Norm heading her way. *Oh, no, the hedgehog,* she inwardly groaned. It took all of her self-control to keep from yanking the ridiculous hairpiece from his head. Instantly she grabbed a stack of files and snatched up a pen.

"Hello, Mel," he greeted, his teeth gleaming like a toothpaste commercial.

She raised her head and crinkled her forehead. "Oh, hi, Norm."

"Busy?"

"Extremely," she replied, lowering her eyes to the papers before her. "Did you need something?"

"No. Looks like Jackie likes her flowers." He leaned against her door with his chubby fingers hooked inside his belt.

Melanie forced a smile and momentarily cast her gaze in his direction. "Yes, she thanked me."

"Are you ready for another cup of coffee? We have about fifteen minutes before opening."

She sighed. "No, thank you. I really have had enough."

He cleared his throat. "Wilson Anderson and I have a meeting at the downtown branch until noon, but I wondered if you had plans for lunch?"

"Yes, I do. I'm sorry." *No, thanks, Norm, not again.*

He nodded and continued smiling. "We'll just make it another time. Wouldn't want the others to think we had something going."

"Of course not." She bit back a nasty retort. "Have a good morning."

As Norm waddled away, the idea of spending any more time with him nauseated her. If his alliance didn't seem so invaluable, she'd tell him to get lost. Between him and Jackie, she'd soon be accused of lowering her standards. Of course, in the end the rewards would far outnumber the temporary unpleasantness.

The morning flew by until she saw Jackie leave for lunch. A short while later, Melanie grabbed a few files and headed for the other office. Switching on Jackie's computer, she quickly changed its time to ten-thirty that morning when the olive-skinned young woman had been in her office. Once the clock had been altered, she opened Jackie's E-mail and began to type.

Wilson,

After working a week with Miss Copeland, I find her performance is less than satisfactory. She fails to coop- erate during training and is constantly chatting on the phone. On more than one occasion, I needed to show

*her basic computer skills which hindered our work
progress. She has a definite haughty attitude toward the
customers, and I've had to intervene with apologies on
two separate occasions. I don't believe she is the level of
professionalism required at Today's Bank. I felt this
information needed to be called to your attention.*

Jackie Mason

After sending the message, Melanie exited E-mail and
reset the computer's clock.

Bring in the clowns, she thought excitedly, as a tingle
raced up her spine. Her mind spun with the strategy she'd
cleverly put together. *Jackie, you should have never gotten in
my way—not with Wilson Anderson and not with Reed.*

ten

"Okay, Sis, should I get the yellow or green sleeper?" Shanna asked, displaying an infant outfit in each hand. The sisters had decided to meet at a baby boutique during Jackie's lunch hour and utilize a generous gift certificate given to Shanna at a recent baby shower.

Jackie wrinkled her nose. "They're both darling, but I'd rather you wait until after the baby is born."

"And let Jeff pick out the going-home outfit?"

Jackie laughed at the horrified look on Shanna's round face. "He might surprise you, but truthfully, I want to buy it—in pink or blue."

Shanna grinned, her brown eyes sparkling. She hung the sleepers, complete with matching blankets, back on the rack. "Deal." She patted her tummy affectionately. "See, darling, Aunt Jackie will make sure you are dressed properly."

Giggling, the two browsed through the store, admiring all the baby clothes and accessories.

"Mom told me you had a date this past weekend." Shanna examined a package of terry-cloth bibs.

Jackie shook her head in disbelief. "News sure travels fast. And yes, I did have a date."

Shanna's gaze lifted, reflecting her amusement. "Are you going to tell me all about it?"

Jackie shrugged, pretending interest in a white wicker bassinet. "Well, his name is Reed Parker. Remember, you met him at the restaurant?"

"Um, yes, the good-looking one who rescued you from that jerk."

Jackie moistened her lips while considering what to tell Shanna about Reed. "He's a Christian, very nice, and attentive."

"Which tells me you like him."

"Oh, kinda."

"Wow, Sis, you haven't been interested in anyone for a long time," Shanna pointed out. "What makes this guy special?"

"Everything." Jackie laughed. "I know it's a little early to make a hasty decision, especially since he probably has some horrible fault lurking about." She sighed, purposely placing her hand over her heart. Shanna laughed.

"From the look on your face, I don't think it matters."

"What look?" Jackie feigned irritation.

Shanna peered into her sister's face, then pointed. "The dreamy one I see in your eyes. Right there with Venus and the stars."

"That evident?" Jackie cringed, touching her cheek.

Shanna nodded. "Hopeless. Might as well tell me when you're planning to see him again."

She grinned. "Tomorrow night at the premier of Paul's play."

"Oh, so soon?" Shanna smiled, walking toward the check-out counter. "We're going, too. I'm anxious to see the product of our little brother's directing. Of course, now I have another reason—interrogating your date."

"Go easy on him," Jackie warned disapprovingly. "He really is shy."

"Shy? He won't stand a chance with our crew."

"Just hush." Jackie laughed. "He's already met the kids, and did just fine."

Shanna glanced at her watch. "You'd better scoot if you plan to get back to work on time."

"Guess so." Jackie pulled up her jacket sleeve to verify the time. She tried to give Shanna a hug, but couldn't find a comfortable way to reach around her bulging stomach.

"Give it up," Shanna grumbled, "at least for another three weeks. I'll see you tomorrow night at the high school."

Settling for giving her sister a loving pat on the shoulder and a kiss on the cheek, Jackie hurried from the boutique, feeling incredibly happy. She pulled her keys from her purse along with a chocolate-peanut bar. *I'll get some orange juice from the break room,* she promised herself, tearing open the wrapper. Moments later, candy bar in mouth, she left the baby boutique's parking lot en route to the bank.

God, You are so good. Thank You for all of Your wonderful blessings.

Back in her office, Jackie returned a few phone calls and scheduled closings for two home loans. A woman stopped in to co-sign on her son's application for an auto loan, and a young married couple asked for information in obtaining funds to purchase furniture. Midafternoon the phone rang.

"Commercial loans," she answered lightly.

"Jackie, this is Wilson Anderson. Can you come to my office, please?" His voice held an edge.

"Sure, I'll be right up." Gathering up a notepad, she hurried down the hall, wondering what the vice president needed.

Upstairs in Wilson's office, Jackie took a seat across from his desk. He seemed concerned about something. Tiny lines framed the lower corners of his eyes. Facing her solemnly, he folded his hands on the desktop.

"I've got a problem," he said grimly.

She met his gaze—questioning, wondering.

"I received your E-mail."

Puzzled, Jackie shook her head. "I didn't send you any today."

He stared at her thoughtfully. "It originated from your computer and was sent while you were here this morning."

"I don't understand," she began, searching her memory to see if she'd neglected something. "Nothing's been sent. . .not even a copy or forward."

He sighed, and she viewed the muscles twitch in his jaw.

"What's wrong?" she asked with mounting uneasiness.

He stood and shut the door to his office. Sitting back down, he paused before speaking. "As I said before, I have a problem. Tell me, have you had any difficulties with Melanie Copeland?"

Shocked at his unusual question, Jackie replied. "Absolutely none. She's friendly and committed to the bank. I think her professionalism will be an asset to the business."

"Then why did you send this to me?" He lifted a copy of an E-mail and handed it to her.

Jackie slowly read the message. She couldn't believe her eyes! Who could have done this to Melanie? Somebody obviously had a problem with the new loan officer. She reread the top of the page; it *had* come from her PC at a time in which she'd been working in her office. In fact, she remembered taking an application then.

"If this is a joke, it's not funny," she stated, handing the sheet of paper back to him. "I didn't compose this, and it's certainly not true."

Wilson raked his fingers through his sandy-colored hair. "The wording isn't your style, either. Do you know of anyone who may have something against you or Miss Copeland?"

Jackie hesitated, thinking through the past week and all that had transpired with Melanie's training and the other employees. Everyone had been helpful and considerate. Shaking her head, she replied. "No. . .not at all. How could this have happened? I mean, it did come from my computer."

He exhaled and placed his hands behind his head. "The origination is easy enough. Someone could simply get into your PC, change the time, send me this E-mail, and then correct the clock."

"Why?" she asked incredulously.

"I thought you might be able to shed a little light on the matter." He regarded her through narrowed blue eyes.

She willed her trembling hands to stop shaking. "I honestly have no idea. It definitely upsets me."

"I can tell." Wilson studied the message again. "Jackie, do me a favor and don't mention this incident to anyone else. If we have an employee who believes he or she has gotten away with a prank, the troublemaker may try again."

Jackie wet her lips. The thought of a coworker purposely damaging her or Melanie's credibility infuriated her. "I plan to keep my eyes open."

"Smart idea. Frankly, it looks like a case of jealousy. One

of the other employees might have wanted Miss Copeland's position."

She shook her head. "It doesn't make sense to me."

Wilson folded the paper and dropped it into the trash beside his desk. "I'm speculating, but if my hunch is correct, our culprit may try for round two."

She brushed her clammy hands together. "The whole thing makes me nervous and angry."

"And suspicious," he added dryly.

Shortly afterward, Jackie descended the stairs to her office. She found it difficult to concentrate on her work. In the seven years she'd been with Today's Bank, nothing had ever happened like this. Why would anyone want to discredit a new employee, especially one who worked as hard as Melanie? In addition, the E-mail was a bad reflection on Jackie.

Maybe one of the other staff persons did desire Melanie's position, but what if that someone had a problem with Jackie as well? As the afternoon progressed, she began to study every secretary, teller, and officer who happened to pass by her office. *This is wrong!* she told herself. *These people are decent and loyal. How can I possibly distrust any of them?*

While her mind continued to deliberate over the conversation with Wilson, a growing ache moved across the top of her head. Soon the pain extended down to her right ear and neck. Even her teeth hurt. With a sigh, she acknowledged she had a migraine.

Suddenly every voice, click of a heel, or rustling paper was magnified, causing her head to vibrate. She fumbled for her keys to unlock the desk drawer containing the prescription medicine for emergencies like these. Suddenly a jolt of pain pierced Jackie's right eye, as though someone twisted a knife inside it.

Taking a deep breath, she attempted to unlock the drawer, but the key refused to slide into the allotted slot. *Please, God, help me with this,* she prayed, realizing at any moment tears would flow. In the next instant, the key slipped into the opening, and she secured the medication.

Frustration rippled through her when the cellophane seal containing a single dose of medicine wouldn't budge. Reaching for her letter opener, she inadvertently turned over a cold cup of coffee. Jackie prayed for control. All the while, the incessant pain snapped at her senses. Finally, the letter opener punctured the wrapper, and she tore into its contents.

As she swallowed the medicine, Jackie suddenly noticed Melanie curiously watching her on the other side of the glass wall. Jackie squinted through blurry eyes to see the woman. Melanie glared back, seemingly enthralled with the sight before her. A derisive grin played upon her lips.

Jackie squeezed her eyes shut. She didn't care about Melanie's response to her agony—only that the pain would stop. When she opened her eyes again, the woman had disappeared.

Jackie felt a tightening knot in the pit of her stomach. Occasionally, the migraines brought on vomiting, but this didn't feel the same. The twisting inside her came from shock. . .and trepidation. Surely Melanie wouldn't revel in watching her suffer. It must be a mistake. Maybe Jackie only thought she saw her new coworker. Sometimes her headaches caused her vision to play games with her mind.

Then again, Reed's apprehension could be right.

❧

Reed hung up Yukon's leash and patted his pet's head. "We had a good run, didn't we, fella?" After filling the dog's water dish, he snatched up the portable phone with one hand and a quart bottle of sparkling water with the other. Sinking into his green leather recliner, he drank half the contents. Glancing over at Yukon lapping the water, he laughed. "I've got it bad, Yukon. Can't get the lady off my mind. I'm even beginning to think in terms of 'we' instead of 'I.' "

Punching in Jackie's number, he settled back in his chair and eagerly anticipated her sweet voice.

"Hello."

Reed frowned. She sounded sleepy. "Jackie?"

"Hi, Reed."

She definitely sounded groggy. "Did I wake you?"

"No, I'm resting on the couch."

"Everything okay?"

"Oh, yeah. I had a headache earlier, but it's going away."

"Are you sure? You don't sound very chipper to me."

"Honestly, I'm feeling much better. The medication I took makes me sleepy."

"Must be a migraine," he said with a sigh. "I can come over and take care of you—fix you an ice pack or massage your head."

She laughed lightly. "Now you sound like my mother."

He chuckled. "Oops, don't want to fill that role. Did you have a bad day at work?"

"Sorta."

"Do you want to talk about it?"

"Not tonight, but thank you. I want to sort through my thoughts first. We may need to discuss it tomorrow evening, if the offer still holds."

He could feel the warmth in her voice. "Of course it does." He paused. *Wonder if Melanie is up to her old tricks?* "Seven o'clock okay with you?"

"Yes, perfect, and I apologize for this headache business."

He smiled into the phone. "You just take care of yourself. Well, good night, pretty lady. Crawl into bed and chase away your headache."

"Um, I believe I'll follow your advice. Thanks for calling. Bye."

Reed sat for several minutes, contemplating Jackie's unpleasant afternoon. A helpless feeling settled over him. He wanted to fix whatever hadn't gone right for his girl. *His girl.* Already he considered Jackie his. *Be careful,* he cautioned himself. *Don't want to suffocate her or scare her away.* He needed to let God advance their relationship, and Him alone. But he couldn't help but worry that Melanie was the root of the day's problems.

Yukon laid his head in Reed's lap. He stroked the animal's head. "I need to pray for a ton of things eating at me—Jackie's health, our relationship, and as hard as it may be, for Melanie and my attitude toward her. It's too easy for me to forget God looks at her in love, just as He does me. It's even harder for me to place all my troubles in His hands."

Setting his water bottle on Sunday's newspaper, he picked up his Bible. He didn't need to consider what he should read; his fingers leafed right to the passage, Psalm 37. Every verse spoke to him, but his gaze fixed on verse 23: "If the LORD delights in a man's way, he makes his steps firm; though he stumble, he will not fall, for the LORD upholds him with his hand."

Still, wariness crept over him each time he pondered Melanie working alongside Jackie.

eleven

"Tell me, what's the name of this play we're seeing tonight?" Reed asked as he turned his Blazer onto Route 51 and headed southeast toward Elmore High School.

Jackie gave him a wry grin. "*One Flew Over the Cuckoo's Nest,* and Paul's directing it." She watched his amused reaction and burst into laughter. "Rather ironic, don't you think? I mean, with what I've told you about my brother's weird sense of humor."

Reed chuckled. "This is the brother who convinced his little sister Olivia that a dinosaur slept under her bed?"

"Same one."

"And got her to leave peanut butter and jelly sandwiches for it to eat at night?"

"That's my brother Paul."

"Didn't he accidentally free a dozen white mice in your parents' home, then decide he could record their habits for a school project?"

"Yes. He was fourteen and a freshman in high school at the time."

"The one who believed his destiny was to be a shark breeder?"

"My brother." Jackie giggled. "Now he wants to direct movies about reptiles of the South American jungles."

Reed reached for her hand and laughed with her. "Whew! Are we expecting any surprises tonight?"

"Let's hope not. His drama teacher and my parents have threatened him within an inch of his life. My guess, he's worked hard to make the play a success. Paul is an all-or-nothing person. When he sets out with a goal, he follows through—no matter what the outcome. I'm just thankful he's adjusted from the rebellion we saw a couple years ago."

Reed lifted a brow. "Realized his way didn't offer any hope for the future?"

"Yeah. He found Jesus at a church camp two summers ago. Although he still withdraws from us when he's upset, he's come a long way."

"Some of his reactions are due to his age." Reed lightly squeezed her hand. "If Paul turns out half as great as his big sister, he'll be prize material."

She felt herself grow warm with the compliment. "Thanks; you're sweet. But I have a ton of faults, which I'm sure you will find out soon enough."

"Doubt it." He paused. "I've been wondering. Did you have a better day than yesterday?"

Jackie heard the sincerity in his gentle voice and appreciated his concern. "Yes, much better." She sighed. "Wilson Anderson, the vice president, asked that I not speak to the other employees about this, but I'd like to tell you what happened. Of course," she said, placing her other hand on his, "it shows I don't handle stress very well."

He smiled and winked. "Ah, one of those fault things. Should I take notes?"

"Please don't; you'll end up filling a notebook."

"Okay, I'll go easy on you." Then more seriously, he added, "Go ahead and tell me, because I don't like anything upsetting you."

Jackie took a deep breath. "Well, I had a great morning, especially after the wonderful weekend." She saw an easy smile upon his lips. "The problems didn't begin until mid-afternoon. . ."

When she finished relaying the mystery of the E-mail message, she turned to study him. "I don't know if I overreacted to the whole matter or not, but I've never had anyone purposely try to involve me in petty employee quarrels. Still, I wish I knew if the one who sent the E-mail intended to damage my credibility or Melanie's."

Reed swallowed hard. "It's really hard to tell. Perhaps jealously is a motive."

She nodded. "Wilson suggested that, too."

"What I don't like is Melanie's reaction to your headache," he commented, as though struggling to control his anger.

Jackie nibbled on her lower lip, contemplating the whole incident. "I could have possibly misinterpreted it."

He glanced over at her. "She's capable of just about anything. Don't underestimate her."

"Even if she's a Christian?"

"I have my doubts about that," Reed replied impassively.

Jackie failed to respond. It went against everything Jackie believed in to doubt Melanie's faith. "Why?" she finally asked. "You seem so sure."

"I'm more than sure. In fact, I'm positive. Let me tell you about her phone call to me last Friday night."

Once he recounted the story, she stared out the window. She felt overwhelmed.

"Do you have a solution?" Jackie asked quietly, studying his profile.

His handsome features were drawn and tense. "None, except to be careful."

She pondered his request. "I'm having a difficult time making sense of this. What reasons would she have to say she's a Christian?"

Reed shrugged. "Motive? It depends upon her driving force. You and I have the Lord to walk with us through life. Others use money, power, or fame. Unbelievers behave like unbelievers. You can't expect more."

"Except I never told her about my faith."

"You asked the blessing before we ate lunch," Reed reminded her.

Jackie nodded thoughtfully. "So you think Melanie decided then to claim she's a Christian?"

"Perhaps," he slowly replied. "I'd rather think she knew your beliefs beforehand. Melanie is cunning and clever. She never used to act impulsively—always thought out everything to her advantage."

"But who would have told her?" As soon as the words left

her mouth, a picture of Norm Timmons flashed across her mind. "Oh, Reed, I just had a thought. The supervisor over Melanie and me is quite taken with her. He could have offered the information. But I hate to point an accusing finger."

"We're not judging Melanie or blaming her. What we are doing is discussing the circumstances and coming up with some possible answers. Who knows? Yesterday could have been an isolated incident with the E-mail and her reaction to your migraine."

"Right," Jackie quickly agreed. "Guess I need to pray for Melanie and whoever used my computer. And I'm going to be extremely cautious. I know I'm naive—another one of my faults." She took a deep breath. "But I'm not stupid."

"That's my girl." He hesitated. "Do you mind that connotation—'my girl'?"

"No, not at all." Feeling a little bolder, she continued. "In fact, I like it."

He stared at the road ahead, as if searching for the right words. "I really do care for you, Jackie. I realize it's soon, but I needed to say it. If I'm suffocating you, let me know."

"I will. . .but you're not. And I feel the same about you," she answered after a brief hesitation. "It's a little scary, isn't it?"

He flashed her a grin. "Yeah. Me, the confirmed bachelor who had no intention of ever dating again. You've had me turning cartwheels since we met."

She laughed nervously. "I've been content for years as a career-minded woman. Now my thoughts are heading in another direction."

Jackie sensed their relationship was moving ahead a bit too fast, like riding a roller coaster straight down without seeing the track level out. Since the first time Reed inquired about a construction loan, he'd been special. Everything about him attracted her—his quiet manners, sincere humility, his undeniable good looks, and his little-boy grin. He demonstrated his care and concern for her in every breath. She wondered if she deserved such a wonderful man.

It was no big surprise to Jackie that Melanie would want him back. Oddly enough, if Melanie hadn't broken their engagement, she and Reed would be married right now. Obviously the two had shared a lot together, and some of those things Reed didn't appear to be too proud about. But now he knew the Lord. When Jackie stopped to think about that, having Jesus in his life was Reed's best attribute.

❧

Reed instantly spotted the Mason family in the school's lobby. In truth, how could he miss them? He recognized Shanna from the restaurant and the others from the afternoon at the park. A slightly plump woman with short, snow-white hair waved in Jackie and Reed's direction, and he saw a grin spread over the face of a middle-aged man. As he and Jackie moved closer to her family, the boys shouted to Reed.

"Ron Mason," Jackie's dad immediately greeted, offering Reed a handshake. "Glad you could come out tonight."

Reed gazed into the warm gray eyes of the tall, thin man and introduced himself. "It's a pleasure, sir."

"And this is my mother, Nita Mason," Jackie said.

The older woman released one hand from Lacy's wheelchair and grasped Reed's. "I'm so glad to meet you," she stated. "And I want to thank you for spending time with the kids a couple of Saturdays ago."

"Thank you," Reed replied, noticing how both of Jackie's parents made him feel comfortable and not the least bit shy. "I enjoyed them. They're a great bunch."

"I've heard good things about you," Ron declared with a chuckle. "Although more from the kids than from my daughter."

"Oh, Dad." Jackie blushed. Reed thought she looked lovelier than before. To save her from more embarrassing comments, he asked, "Are you sure it was me they talked about, or my dog?" He glanced accusingly at the kids standing nearby and winked.

"Oh, you, absolutely," Nita interjected. "Of course, they enjoyed your pet, too."

Reed chuckled and nodded at the boys. "You fellas ready

for this great play?"

They weren't quite sure.

He bent to Lacy's eye level. "Hello, pretty lady. It's good to see you again," he said softly, patting her red hair. She tilted her head and gave him a sideways grin.

Rising, Reed spotted Olivia, her blond hair in deep contrast to her darker-skinned brothers. "Are you keeping those boys in line?"

"You bet," she informed him proudly. And he didn't doubt it for an instant.

"Great family you have here," Reed said to the Masons. He admired and respected what they were doing in adopting hard-to-place children. It took special people to face the challenges accompanying any kind of physical or mental handicap. Jackie's folks were so much like his parents. Too bad he'd been such a stinker, or they'd have adopted a whole tribe.

They entered the high school auditorium and found seats near the front. Reed enjoyed the play, and Paul did a splendid job directing. Once the curtain fell on the performance, the African-American youth joined them. A smile appeared to be engraved across his face.

"If you didn't have school tomorrow, we'd celebrate," Ron said. "You did a great job, Son." He placed a hand on Paul's shoulder. "Saturday night, after the last show, I'll plan something. What would you like?"

The young man beamed. "Pizza, lots of it. And could Reed come, too?"

His father glanced at his daughter's guest. "It's up to you. We'd love to have you join us."

"Wouldn't miss it," Reed replied. "I'll be here."

Later, in the darkness of his apartment, Reed reflected on the evening and the Mason family. At first he'd felt uneasy about meeting Jackie's parents, but it took only a short while for him to relax. He respected the way Ron and Nita managed their children, constantly building them up—praising and encouraging them. Being with the Masons reminded him of the year he volunteered with severely challenged children. He'd been impressed with the love he'd seen doctors and nurses lavish on the children, and tonight he'd viewed that same tender spirit in the Masons.

Before the play started, after the initial introductions were made, he'd run out of things to say. Jackie must have perceived his nervousness, for she'd hooked her arm into his and offered to give him a tour of the high school. He could get used to a woman like Jackie—permanently. Imagine waking every morning to those gorgeous hazel eyes and that sweet personality. . .

His mind drifted back to Jackie's concern about the day before, especially Melanie's response to her migraine. Unfortunately, he knew Melanie's capabilities.

Lord, please watch out for my girl, he prayed. *Protect her from all danger. And Lord, if I'm wrong about Melanie, make it so clear that I'd have to be a fool to ignore it. If my suspicions are true, Melanie needs You in her life.*

twelve

Melanie toyed with the key in her hand. It belonged to Jackie's office, and she'd had it copied during those first few days they'd worked together. At the time, Melanie thought it might come in handy, and this morning it would. The idea had come to her some days before, but she had to wait until just the precise moment to act.

Arriving at the bank early, she met Norm making coffee in the break room. From their breakfast together the morning she bought Jackie's flowers, she knew he used two teaspoons of sugar and one of cream. She purposely waited and fixed his coffee, handing it to him with a sweet smile. By chatting with him before excusing herself to catch up on the mounting paperwork, Melanie knew she'd succeeded in charming him. Once she saw Norm head to his office, she quietly unlocked Jackie's door.

A stack of file folders lay on the right-hand corner of her desk. Melanie had observed Jackie's habit of putting the most pertinent work always on that corner. Melanie pulled out two files and went back to her office. Once behind her closed door, she pulled out three of her own files and together with Jackie's shoved them inside her briefcase.

She giggled. This might bring on another headache for dear Miss Goody-goody. If this incident didn't, the one she planned for the following week would certainly reduce her to a whimpering puppy. Very soon, Melanie must make a trip to Wilson's office. . .and lay the groundwork.

❧

Jackie inhaled the fresh smell of spring. Even in the city, shoots of green pushed their way through the ground as though saying "notice me." Of course, songwriters called this the season of love. And she'd definitely fallen in love with Reed Parker.

What a joke on me, she mused. Before Reed, she'd given up on relationships and chosen to focus her energies on God. And now what a blessing He'd given her!

Work had been good all week, with no problems or glitches. Melanie continued to be sweet, and they'd even gone to lunch on Wednesday. Melanie had no family; she'd been the only child of an older couple who had long since passed away. Jackie wanted to befriend the lonely young woman, if for no other reason than to prove her own suspicions wrong.

Once she unlocked her office, she flipped on her computer and checked her E-mail. Several home loans had been approved, including Reed's. She still received the real estate listing, although his loan was her only responsibility.

Jackie picked up the phone and tapped in his number. He answered it on the first ring.

"Good morning," she greeted.

"Hey, sunshine," he replied softly.

Jackie loved the sound of his voice. "I've got good news for you."

"You're coming to work for General Motors?"

"No." She laughed softly. "But your home loan has been approved—not that I had any doubts."

"Wonderful," he claimed. "Can't wait to talk to the contractor."

"Well, I believe your days of apartment living may be numbered."

"What a blessing," he said with a chuckle. "How about celebrating over lunch? After all, I haven't seen you since Tuesday and this is Thursday."

She felt a tingle from her head to her toes. "I imagine it could be arranged."

"Um, just the two of us," he said tenderly. "Do you like Chinese food?"

"Love it."

"There's a restaurant near you, but I can't think of the name."

"Flying Dragon?" Jackie asked.

"That's it. Shall we say twelve-fifteen?"

"Okay. Why don't I meet you there instead of you taking the time to come in after me?" *And that guarantees we won't have any unexpected company.*

"It's a date."

Jackie laid the receiver into its cradle and mentally calculated the hours until she'd see Reed again. Wonderful, wonderful man. Last night, they'd talked for hours on the phone, discussing everything from childhood memories to favorite vacation spots. She respected the fact he didn't always agree with her and had definite opinions of his own. He held excellent views and insights into subjects she didn't understand—like world trade.

She shook her head to clear her mind for the work on her desk. Pulling a stack of files from the right-hand corner of her desk, she began reading the attached Post-it notes, acting on each directive.

At ten o'clock she received a call from a woman who wanted to close her auto loan in the morning. Confirming a time with the customer, she sorted through the files. Missing. Frustrated, she looked again, but to no avail. Jackie whirled around to the credenza behind her, but the missing file wasn't there either.

She searched her memory for another possible spot. Finally Jackie decided to resume the search after lunch, certain the file had to be on her desk. She'd have to find it shortly, because the contract must be typed with the correct interest rate, date, and figures.

Shortly before eleven, she looked for another file that had been with the other missing one. Puzzled, Jackie decided the two must have been misfiled together. But she had long ago established a routine with the customers' paperwork and had no reason to deviate from it.

"Jackie?"

She glanced up to see Melanie wearing a worried frown.

"Do you have a minute?"

"Sure, what's up?" Jackie asked, relieved to put aside her dilemma.

Melanie sat in a chair in front of the desk and wet her lips. "I don't know how it happened, but I have three files missing from my desk. I wouldn't be alarmed if only one couldn't be found; however, three is a bit much. I'm not sure what to do." She shifted uncomfortably. "Norm and Wilson will think I'm completely incompetent."

"No, they won't," Jackie said gently. All the while her mind spun with alarm and worry. . .the E-mail message last week and now this. Wilson had spoken the truth when he predicted the culprit might strike again. "Don't worry, Melanie. Let me look into the matter. To be perfectly honest, I just discovered two files missing from my desk."

Melanie's mouth flew open. "Why would anyone want to take customer files? Oh, my, there's confidential information in them. We could get into a lot of trouble."

Jackie took a deep breath and rose from her chair. "I'm going to see Wilson."

"Shouldn't we talk to Norm first?" Melanie asked, her ice blue eyes watering. "I feel terrible."

Jackie stared at the distressed woman and felt a growing sense of empathy. "You go on back to your office, and I'll be in once I speak with Wilson."

Melanie attempted a smile, but her lips quivered. "Do you want me to accompany you? After all, we both have the same problem."

"No," Jackie replied. "If I need you, I'll call."

After Melanie left, Jackie stood and searched once more for the missing records. She crossed her arms and glanced down at her desk. *I need to focus on the Problem Solver, not the problem,* she told herself. *There's an explanation for this, and I refuse to let it upset me. At least I now know Melanie isn't the troublemaker. What a relief!*

Determined, she rang the vice president's office. His secretary answered.

"Hi, Carla, this is Jackie. Is Wilson busy?"

"Um, don't think so. I'll transfer the call."

Jackie drummed her fingers on her desk, asking God to give her peace and wisdom to handle the situation properly.

"Good morning, Jackie."

"Good morning. Do you have time to talk with me? Seems our 'friend' may have been busy."

He sighed. "Come on up. I was afraid we might have trouble again, and my gut feelings are usually right."

Moments later, seated in the vice president's office, Jackie explained the situation.

"Both of you are missing vital files?" He shook his head in apparent disgust. "And we pride ourselves on customer confidentiality."

"I'm really sorry," Jackie stated.

"Well, I'm certain it's not your fault. You and Miss Copeland will have a rough job of reconstructing the paperwork."

She nodded. The thought infuriated her.

He paused and tapped his pen on the desk. His dark blue gaze bore into hers. "I'm going to have the locks changed on your offices. I should have seen to it last week. Frankly, it didn't occur to me at the time."

"An excellent idea," Jackie said. "And it should stop the pranks."

"I don't like this," he muttered with a frown. "We screen our employees carefully." He glanced up at Jackie. "Why are you being targeted? You're one of the best we have and certainly the most amiable."

"I have no idea who or why," Jackie answered, feeling his frustration at the same level of hers.

"Well, God knows," he pointed out quietly.

Jackie smiled. "I keep telling myself that He's in control."

"Good." He returned the smile. "We'll just put the matter into His capable hands and act upon His direction."

After the meeting, Jackie went straight to Melanie's office and explained Wilson's plans to change the locks on their doors. Fortunately, the locksmith would be at the bank within the hour. The information brought a sense of security, hopefully not false.

At twelve o'clock, the locksmith still hadn't arrived. With a heavy sigh, Jackie asked herself if it were wise to leave the bank. No one had said whether she needed to stay in her office when the serviceman installed the new locks, and Wilson had left on an appointment. She stood in her doorway, wondering what to do.

"You haven't gone to lunch yet?" Melanie asked, approaching Jackie from the break room with a salad and a diet soda.

"Not yet. I'm not sure if I should leave with the locksmith on his way."

"Don't worry about it." Melanie smiled. "After you talked to Wilson this morning, the least I can do is keep an eye out for the work he ordered. Besides, I'm staying right here for lunch."

Jackie tilted her head. "Are you sure? I feel like this is an imposition."

Melanie's light blue eyes widened. "You lost two files; I lost three. I think I have more at stake than you. If it stops whoever pulled this dirty trick, I'll gladly give up a week of lunch hours."

"All right," Jackie agreed, snatching up her purse. "Thanks. I'll see you later." *She is a good friend, despite Reed's doubts about her faith,* Jackie decided. Then she remembered the phone call Melanie made to Reed last Friday. *Perhaps a little misguided, but she has a good heart.*

❧

Melanie sauntered back into her office. She'd been pondering the problem with the lock changes all morning. At least now she stood a chance of doing something about it.

Right after Jackie left, the serviceman arrived. He appeared to be in his twenties, dark hair and eyes. Not too bad-looking, Melanie determined. The receptionist had escorted him back to her area and listened while Melanie explained which doors were to have the work completed. She watched the receptionist traipse back to her area in the lobby. The woman liked nothing better than sitting in the front of the bank and scrutinizing everyone who entered, like a bird in a cage. How boring.

The locksmith began in the empty office. Melanie set her food aside and applied lipstick before heading his way. She glanced around; luckily, the desks around them were deserted.

"How are you today?" she asked, stopping right in front of him where his eyes could trail down her short skirt. No matter what the man did for a living, he would be sure to have the characteristics of a normal male.

"Just fine, thank you," he said, failing to look her way.

"Do you think the job will take very long?"

"Naw, probably less than ten minutes each. Is this your office?"

"No, mine is two doors down, the other one to be changed."

The man paused and stood from his kneeling position. "I'm not sure what to do with the master key. I understand Mr. Anderson is gone for lunch."

Melanie inwardly thrilled at the prospect. "Oh, don't worry about that. I'll be glad to give it to him."

"Okay, thanks," he said with a smile. "I'll be right over to your office. Do I leave the keys for this office with you, too?"

"Sure," she agreed pleasantly, noticing the gold band on his left hand and speculating over what kind of daft woman would be interested in a service-oriented person. She detested his blue one-piece overall with the words "Toledo Locksmith" neatly stitched across his heart. Oh well, she didn't need to impress him any longer, and she walked back to her office to finish lunch.

By my wits, I will succeed, she vowed. *This lady doesn't need anyone but herself.* She considered Jackie and her reliance upon a so-called God. *You are so stupid, Miss Goody-goody, and so is Wilson Anderson for believing in the same nonsense. Let's see your religion save you from what I have in store for both of you.*

When the serviceman left twenty minutes later, she placed Jackie's new key on her desk with a note.

All done! Here's the new key. Looks like we're in business again. Hope you had a nice lunch.

Melanie

thirteen

"Time to read our fortune cookies," Reed announced, offering Jackie one of the Chinese treats from a small plate.

"All right," Jackie said, promptly selecting one. "Who goes first?"

"Why, the lady, of course," he replied with a smile. Their hour together had flown by as they feasted on wonton soup, egg rolls with sweet-and-sour sauce, and a buffet of various Chinese dishes.

Jackie broke open her cookie and silently read.

"I'm waiting," he coaxed, attempting to peer across the table at the piece of paper dangling from her hand. "Hope I paid the owner enough to stuff the right fortune into your cookie."

Smiling, she stared across the table into his handsome face. He'd worn a teal-colored polo shirt that accented his dark complexion. "You are incorrigible," she whispered, sitting straighter in the chair and waving the tiny missive as though making a royal proclamation.

"Shall I call for a drumroll?" he asked, his brown eyes dancing mischievously.

"No, sir. That won't be necessary. I'll read it to you. . .it says, 'You have a secret admirer.'"

"Are the initials CRP on the bottom?"

She shook her head. "I think it's anonymous. What does the 'C' stand for?"

He grinned. "Christopher."

"Um, Christopher Reed Parker. Nice name."

"Thanks. My mother's idea, you know."

"Usually parents are the ones who name their children."

"Oh, you are such a clever woman," he stated with a chuckle. "Now, what is your full name?"

She sighed and rolled her eyes. Her middle name had

plagued her since she'd entered kindergarten. "It's not pretty."

"Has to be if it belongs to you. I started out being called 'Chrissy' until my dad declared I'd be 'Reed.'"

"Okay," she laughed. "It's Jacquelyn Danae."

A look of shock spread across his face. "It's a beautiful name!"

"Not if the kids called you Jackie Tooth Decay."

They shared another laugh then realized they needed to get back to work soon.

"Thanks for celebrating my loan approval with me," he whispered, leaning across the table as they waited for the check.

"My pleasure. I bet you're excited."

He nodded. "I'd thought of little else until you came along. Something about you distracts me, though. Can't seem to figure it out."

"Maybe you should see a doctor," she teased.

"Nope. I think the condition is terminal." He stood from the table. "Are we still on for Saturday night?"

"Of course. Are you sure you're up to another evening with my family?"

He winked. "By all means. Another helping of *One Flew Over the Cuckoo's Nest* is just what I need. Now, what about Sunday church?"

"You bet. Mine or yours?" She tilted her head.

"Well, your parents and my parents attend the same church, right?" he asked slyly.

"Yes. And that's where I worship, too."

"Then let's go to yours and see what kind of gossip we can generate."

The look in his soft brown eyes told her he cared. . . very much. "It's a date." She still felt a little frightened, but oh, so good.

They left the restaurant, and Reed escorted Jackie to her car. She'd not been this happy in a long time. It didn't matter what they did, as long as they were together.

On the way back to the bank, she remembered their earlier

conversation about the missing files.

"Melanie couldn't possibly have been involved with this incident," Jackie had pointed out.

He'd hesitated before responding. "Perhaps I've been wrong." But the look on his face told her otherwise. "Please, Jackie, watch yourself."

Why did he continue to doubt poor Melanie? Had she hurt him so badly that he refused to forgive her?

Oh, Lord, I don't understand the situation between Melanie and Reed. He is so hostile toward her. What am I supposed to do?

❧

Reed watched the Mason kids swallow pizza like they were starved. He could carry his own when it came to eating, but he'd forgotten how much food teenagers consumed.

He enjoyed this family. They were typical. . .and they were not. The kids acted like normal kids; that is, those who were raised to respect each other and their parents. They teased and picked, quarreled and fussed, but what drew him the most was the love filling them up and spilling over. Reed knew Jesus did that to people. Too bad he'd fought it all those years.

Glancing at Jackie, her hazel eyes sparkling and a smile playing upon her sweet lips, he suddenly felt a tremendous urge to tell her he'd fallen in love with her. She'd probably think him nuts, especially since they'd only known each other for a short while. Except Reed knew, without a doubt, that Jacquelyn Danae Mason would one day move into his new home as Mrs. Reed Parker. He'd heard God whisper to him about her, nudge him when she gave him a special look. He prayed she felt the same. Now, if he could only contain his excitement until a proper amount of time passed.

Early Sunday morning, Reed phoned his parents. *Better not to spring too many surprises on them at one time.* He grinned as he heard the phone ring.

"Hi, Mom."

"Well, aren't you the early one?" Doris Parker remarked.

He envisioned his tall, slender, auburn-headed mother making coffee as she prepared breakfast for his dad.

"I'm attending your church this morning," he blurted out, not quite sure how to tell her about Jackie.

"Wonderful!" She called to his dad, "David, Reed's planning to join us for church today."

Reed knew his father would be thrilled and heard him ask, "How about lunch with us afterward?"

"Mom," Reed began, "I'm bringing a girl with me."

"A girl! David, you won't believe this, but he's bringing a girl."

He heard his dad in the background. "What's her name?"

"It's Jackie." Reed laughed. "You know her parents, Ron and Nita Mason."

His mother sniffed happily. "Oh, yes, a beautiful girl and a special family. I'm so happy for you."

Reed shook his head. "Mom, we're not getting married, just coming to church together."

"But it's a start! Will you two have lunch with us?"

"It sounds fine to me, but I need to check with Jackie."

Suddenly his mother sounded even more bubbly. "Goodness, are you planning to sit with the Masons or us? And it doesn't matter; we'll understand."

"Don't know, Mom," he said dryly. "We hadn't talked about where we'd sit. I'll sneak in and then decide. Got to hurry and shower. See you later. Love you and give Dad a hug for me."

Reed hung up the phone and laughed—long and hard. His parents would have him and Jackie married with a dozen kids before they made it to church this morning. He hadn't felt this good in years. True, God had always given him joy, but this happiness came as an unexpected blessing.

But forefront in his mind was Melanie. He didn't trust her and he wished Jackie saw through her "nice girl" facade.

Later, in the middle of the sermon, Reed took a sideways glance at Jackie. She looked lovely, dressed in a royal blue dress and matching blazer. Her long curly hair cascaded down her back. . .perfect in every way.

They had elected to sit with his parents and accept the invitation to lunch. He wanted to tell them about the loan approval and drive them by his little piece of heaven. Jackie hadn't seen it either, and he was anxious for her to view the rolling green property and huge maple trees. He'd planned to have his house built nestled in the shade, with nearly an acre front yard.

Perhaps he could consult her about the many decisions that surrounded building his home. That way she'd be sure to like it.

He gave himself a mental shake and focused his attention on the morning's message. Oddly enough, the pastor based his sermon on 1 Corinthians 13—a passage on love. It made him feel slightly uncomfortable, especially with the entire church noticing Reed and Jackie together. To make matters worse, the Masons had chosen the pew in front of them, which encouraged the boys to grin and gape at their sister and Reed whenever the pastor expounded on the significance of love.

Jackie said nothing, but gently tapped her dad on the shoulder, then pointed to her brothers. Ron Mason silenced them with one stern look. Reed's dad concealed his amusement with a cough rather than a laugh, which prompted his wife to poke him in the ribs.

Maybe attending Jackie's church hadn't been such a great idea.

Hours later, Reed drove Jackie back to Toledo. Lunch and the afternoon with his parents had proved successful, at least in Reed's opinion. He marveled at Jackie's versatility. One minute his dad would question her about the interest rates on home loans, and in the next, his mother asked about Shanna's pregnancy. Reed adored her contagious laughter and sweet voice. In fact he hadn't found anything yet he didn't love.

"You were a good sport today," Reed commented, pulling onto Route 51.

"Oh? And what do you call a good sport?" Jackie teased, her hazel eyes sparkling.

He gave her a quick wink, then turned his attention back to his driving. "I mean, you handled my parents just fine. I can never remember them asking me so many questions."

She laughed. "You forget; I've known them for a long time. They just hadn't seen me with you before. Could it be you were nervous?"

Reed shrugged. "A little."

"Your parents are great, and it's obvious they love you."

"Yeah, they are. Both of them seemed to like the house site."

"Oh, Reed, it's gorgeous. You are so lucky to build your dream home on such a beautiful spot."

He reached to take her hand into his. "Well, I've got a big favor to ask of you."

"Okay, let me hear it, and I'll decide if I can oblige you or not."

He swallowed. Perhaps he should approach the subject of his new home at another time. Too late now. "Actually, I need help selecting things for the house. The builder's going to expect me to pick out everything from the brick to floor coverings. Now, I've got definite opinions about some of it, but decorative things leave me paddling upstream."

"I'd love to help," she quickly stated. "I started out in college wanting to major in interior design, except my love for business and finance took over. I'm not sure my decorating preferences will agree with your tastes, but I'll try."

He let out a sigh and wiped his forehead as though his question had been difficult. In a sense, it had. "Thanks," he said with feigned seriousness. "My mother is into ultra country, and that's not me."

She giggled. "What do you like?"

Reed gave her a puzzled look. "I have no idea."

"Guess you do need help."

They chatted on until entering Toledo. One thing he'd noticed about Jackie, she always had something to add to a conversation.

"Say, do you mind if we stop at my apartment for just a minute? Yukon's been inside all day, and he may need a doggy break."

"I don't mind at all."

"I'll only be long enough to let him out," he replied cautiously, hoping she didn't think he planned to get her into his apartment alone.

She squeezed his hand. "As long as Yukon is around, I'll feel perfectly safe."

He offered a smile. Sometimes the things she didn't say pleased him the most.

As Reed suspected, Yukon met him at the door with the leash in his mouth. Hand in hand, Reed and Jackie walked the dog through the complex grounds, still talking about the day's events. A short while later, they returned to Reed's apartment.

"Mind if I feed him?" he asked, hoping he wasn't keeping her from something important.

Jackie looked up from patting Yukon. "Of course not. Poor thing is probably hungry."

"He's most likely overfed." Reed opened the cupboard above the phone and noticed four messages on his answering machine. "Looks like I'm popular, four phone calls," he said, reaching for the bag of dog food. He pressed the play button and dumped a good amount of food into Yukon's dish. Three of the calls were hang-ups, then suddenly the voice on the answering machine made his mouth turn dry.

"Hi, Reed. I've tried to call you all afternoon. Honey, I can't stand this any longer. I know you've told me that you'd break it off with Jackie, but I hate this deceit. I can't look her in the face on Monday morning knowing we were together Friday. She has to be told about us. I love you, Reed. Please don't put this off any longer."

Reed took a deep breath and exhaled slowly. *I refuse to let Melanie destroy his relationship with Jackie.* He watched Jackie rise from a kneeling position where she'd been playing with the dog. His gaze met her ashen face.

"Did she know you were spending Friday evening with

your sister?" he asked, fighting the overwhelming anger swelling inside him.

Jackie nodded and wet her lips. When she lifted her chin, he could tell she battled tears. . .and what else?

"Melanie cannot be trusted," he said quietly. "She lies until she no longer recognizes the truth."

"Tell me, what's the truth about you two?" She crossed her arms and glared at him accusingly. "Why would Melanie leave a message if you two weren't involved?"

"Jackie," he began, stepping toward her.

She backed up, shaking her head. "Don't touch me."

"Please, believe me," he pleaded. "I would never do anything to hurt you."

Jackie lifted her chin. "Do you tell her the same thing?"

"No, honey. . ."

She waved her hands in front of her. "Don't call me honey. Just take me home."

fourteen

Reed felt like he'd just run straight into a brick wall at the speed of sound. Reduced to rubble, he silently prayed to the Father for guidance. "Jackie, I'll take you home, if that's what you want," he managed. Gazing into her misty, hazel eyes, he breathed deeply. "I have never lied to you. I have no reason to deceive you about anything. If you don't believe me, then ask God. He knows the truth."

With those words, he reached for his keys and followed her to the parking lot. The shadows of evening brought on a chill, or perhaps he felt the coldness of despair. Neither said a word as they walked to the Blazer. Silence seemed to roar and ricochet from the corners of the earth. Jackie opened the passenger door, and Reed walked around to the driver's side and slid behind the wheel. The only sound came from the click as they fastened their seat belts.

Deafening, terminal stillness. Reed refused to bury his love for Jackie beneath the debris of lies and deceit. "Let me ask you this, and you don't have to answer me. If I misled you, would I ask you to seek God's truth?"

When she failed to reply, he stuck the key into the ignition and started up the engine. His anger and frustration threatened to erupt. In times gone by, he'd have allowed rage to control his emotions; now he met his problems with the aid of his Lord.

"I will pray," she finally agreed. "I want to believe you, but I'm confused and. . ."

"Hurt," he completed solemnly. He stole a glimpse at the woman he loved, her troubled face framed in dark brown curls highlighted by the last glimmer of sunset.

She turned away. Perhaps she didn't want him to see her tears. Reed didn't want her to see his, either.

❧

Jackie had tried to sleep since eleven o'clock. Lifting her head from the pillow, she read the neon red numbers on her clock radio: three A.M. Her eyes felt heavy and swollen, and no wonder: She'd cried for hours. Jackie realized she loved Reed, and the thought of his betrayal hurt beyond any conceivable pain. No point in telling herself he didn't matter or she'd recover with no bruises or scars.

True to her word, Jackie had prayed right along with the tears. Now in the black stillness, peace had gently wrapped comfort around her heart and restored her spirit. Even so, she desperately craved the answers to her questions. Whom did she dare trust, Melanie or Reed?

Her thoughts turned to the morning's sermon and the scripture from 1 Corinthians 13, verses 6 and 7: "Love does not delight in evil but rejoices with the truth. It always protects, always trusts, always hopes, always perseveres."

Jackie stared up at the darkened ceiling. Reed had tried to protect her from what he perceived as the truth. On more than one occasion, he'd cautioned her about Melanie and had cited incidents in which she behaved less than a Christian. Jackie recognized his misgivings, and yet she wanted to believe Melanie knew the Lord. Forgiveness put the past to rest and cast sins to the bottom of the sea. Maybe Jackie was naive, but she didn't want to be guilty of judging Melanie.

Searching her memory, she pondered over the times Melanie's actions were less than desirable. After each occurrence, Jackie contributed the woman's reaction to lack of knowledge about the Bible and God's laws. In short, she made excuses for her coworker. Jackie recalled the previous Wednesday when the two had gone to lunch. Melanie had made an inappropriate remark about Jackie and Reed's relationship. Shocked, Jackie had gently explained what God instructed about purity, but Melanie ignored her and simply went on to another topic.

Since Jackie had known Reed, he'd always honored God in his words and actions. What more proof did she need? Without additional contemplation, she picked up the phone and punched in his number. Reed answered on the first ring. Sleep must have evaded him, too.

"Reed."

"Yes."

She felt her tears gather and roll from her eyes. "I trust you. I know you haven't lied to me, and I'm sorry."

"Praise God," he whispered, relief edging his voice.

Jackie hesitated; she had more to say. "I've been making excuses for Melanie, but it won't happen again. I'll continue to pray for her, but I understand now she may still be an unbeliever."

"Good," Reed replied. "I've been lying awake wondering. . ."

She wiped the dampness from her cheeks. "Me, too—praying and crying. I feel awful about this."

"Oh, Jackie, I spent months defending Melanie and blaming myself for the problems in my relationship with her, but it wasn't until I secured my relationship with the Lord that I saw the truth. She is hurting, both spiritually and emotionally. The pain she's caused her parents is heartbreaking."

"And now they're dead."

"What?" he asked incredulously.

"Melanie said her parents had died," Jackie explained. A growing suspicion crept across her mind.

"I talked to them a week ago. They knew Melanie had moved back to Toledo, but she has yet to contact them. Her parents live here, in Ottawa Hills."

Jackie cringed at the deceit. "Oh, my goodness. Why would she make up such a horrible story?"

"Hard to say—shock factor or sympathy. Melanie's parents are good Christian people who love their daughter and want to help her, but she refuses to even see them."

Jackie ran her fingers through her hair. "I don't understand how she manages to hold down a job."

Reed sighed. "Melanie is very intelligent, which is why she's successful in manipulating people."

"And why you cautioned me about her," she added. "I feel so foolish."

"Well, truthfully, I'd hoped she'd changed, too."

Jackie took a deep breath. "Can you forgive me for not trusting you?"

"I already have. Love does that to people."

She heard the tenderness in his voice, and her heart leaped with joy. Not knowing what to say or how to phrase her feelings, she merely uttered, "Thank you."

"Do you think you can sleep now?" he asked.

She smiled. "I'm more awake than before, but I'll try."

"I'll call you tomorrow. Sweet dreams."

"Sweet dreams," she echoed, and replaced the phone in its cradle.

Jackie sighed happily and closed her eyes. Soon, she'd tell him how she felt. After all, love did that to a person.

❧

Before Jackie's call, Reed had tossed and turned, too disturbed to sleep. After they'd hung up the phone, he couldn't sleep because his mind continued to spin like a child's top. Bits of conversation whirled about his head—recollections of Jackie's sincerity and understanding that held hope for the future. He hadn't lost Jackie. If anything, they'd crossed a milestone.

She trusted him.

Reed grinned in the dark. Love and trust went together like. . .peanut butter and jelly. . .bubble gum and bubbles. . . pancakes and syrup. *The pastor sure had a good sermon this morning.*

❧

Jackie smiled and took another wistful look at the dozen, long-stemmed roses gracing the corner of her desk. The florist had delivered them promptly at ten o'clock, nearly an hour ago. Without reading the note, she'd known the sender. They were, by far, the most beautiful deep red blooms imaginable. Their fragrance wafted around her office, lifting her onto the same magic carpet that she always felt she was on with Reed.

Immediately, Jackie had phoned him but got his voice mail. Not wanting to leave a message, she composed an E-mail instead.

Reed,

The roses are lovely, in fact, the most gorgeous I've ever seen. I keep touching them to make sure they are real. Then I pinch myself to make sure I'm not dreaming. What a lucky girl I am!

Thank you so much. . .for everything. Again I'm sorry about our misunderstanding.

Love,
Jackie

Clicking the send button, she sent her missive of love into cyberspace. Staring at the flowers, she smiled happily. *God has surely blessed me with a wonderful man,* she thought, gently touching the tiny white baby's breath mingled with the roses. *Melanie will see it's futile to play games where Reed and I are concerned. I only need to have faith.*

A short while later, a knock on the door interrupted her. Jackie glanced up to see Melanie.

"Hi," Jackie greeted, while a tingle of caution nudged her. "I missed you this morning. Are you okay?"

"Oh, yes. I've been in Norm's office," Melanie replied. She tilted her head. "The roses from Reed?"

Jackie nodded. "Aren't they beautiful?"

"Must be the same florist from years ago," she said with a smile. "Reed is a romantic one, don't you think?"

Jackie swallowed her pride. "Definitely. I'm very fortunate."

Melanie walked to Jackie's desk and leaned over, revealing a less than discreet neckline. "You watch him," she cautioned. "If I didn't care about you, I wouldn't say this but. . .Reed used to have a terrible temper." She flipped back her blond hair from her shoulder. "I'd hate for you to taste his violence."

"I've never seen him angry."

Melanie lifted her chin, accenting her perfectly oval face. "I have the scars to prove it."

Her interest piqued, Jackie closed the file in her hands. "How did it happen?"

Melanie shook her head dramatically, and a frown creased

her delicate features. "A car accident. We were quarreling, and the angrier he got, the faster he drove. I was petrified and begged him to slow down, but he ignored me and pressed harder on the accelerator. When he had to slam on the brakes to keep from hitting a car in front of us, I was thrown into the dashboard."

"Oh, Melanie, I'm so sorry."

She bit her lip and her ice blue eyes grew wide. "I'd feel dreadful if something happened to you."

"I'll be careful," Jackie said gently. "No need to worry about me."

"This is extremely difficult. I mean seeing you, someone I care about, get involved with a man who might not be good for you." With those words, Melanie turned and hurried from the office, leaving Jackie to ponder this new revelation about Reed's temper. Thinking through his response to Melanie's message on his answering machine, Jackie realized Reed might have had a temper at one time, but the Savior must have rescued him from its clutches.

Opening the file on her desk, Jackie checked over the figures for an auto loan closing in twenty minutes. Shortly thereafter, a young couple entered her office to complete the necessary papers.

At noon she waved as Melanie left for lunch. Jackie instantly felt relieved; she didn't relish the thought of spending an hour with her. Although she trusted Reed completely, Melanie's story of his temper plagued her. Was it a lie? She'd simply ask him about it the next time they were together.

Shrugging her shoulders, Jackie worked a few more minutes entering data into her computer. Soon the pangs of hunger took over and she logged out. A hamburger sounded good. Locking her office, she decided to rush out for a quick bite of lunch.

The line at the nearby drive-through forced her to wait longer than she desired for her fast food, but the smell drove her crazy. Finally, with a sandwich, fries, and a diet soda beside her in the car, she headed back to work.

Returning to a still-deserted area of the bank building, Jackie's steps quickened. Reed might have phoned or returned her E-mail. . .but no, she remembered, yesterday he had mentioned a day-long quarterly meeting.

Satisfied that she still had most of the noon hour remaining to enter calculations and updates into her computer, she unlocked her office to enjoy a quiet lunch. Her gaze instantly flew to her roses, but the sight sickened her. Every one of the blooms had been snipped and lay scattered on her desk and floor.

fifteen

Jackie's heart hammered against her chest. She dropped the white lunch bag on the floor. The drink collapsed and spilled, splashing caramel-colored soda all over her hose and shoes.

Who could have done such a thing? Her lovely roses viciously strewn around the room made the pit of her stomach twist into knots. Had jealousy or rage triggered the violence?

How did the culprit gain entrance into her office? She'd locked it when she left and unlocked it when she returned. It didn't make sense. No one else had a key except Wilson—not even Norm.

Too angry to cry, Jackie bent and gathered up the remains of her lunch. Placing the sandwich on her credenza, she tossed the soggy fries and the remains of her drink into the trash. For the first time, she noticed her trembling hands and wobbly knees. The E-mail message to Wilson, the missing files, and Reed's beautiful roses destroyed. When would it end?

Massaging her shivering arms, Jackie realized the problems started when Melanie recognized Reed. Taking a ragged breath, she placed a hand on the corner of her desk. *Oh, heavenly Father, I am afraid. I never thought the day would come when I'd be the victim of someone's depraved mind. Yet, it's happening. I suspect Melanie, but, Lord, I don't want to falsely accuse her of this. I don't want to judge. . .I don't want to have a critical spirit. If I'm to react in love, then show me how. Your Word tells us to be wise as serpents and harmless as doves. Help me, Father; I need Your guidance.*

She glanced down at her soiled shoes and hose, then pulled several tissues from her desk to wipe them. The deep green carpet was splotched with soda; it too needed cleaning. Upon a second look, Jackie saw the wet spots looked like huge tears. She sank into her chair and began to cry. For several minutes she grieved—not the loss of the roses, for they were fleeting, but for the person who had repeatedly attempted to hurt her. Someone despised her, and that person knew how to get into her office.

Suddenly she had an idea. *Thank You, Father.*

Inhaling deeply, she wet her lips and reached for a tissue. First, she must collect herself and look presentable. Rising from the chair, she grabbed her purse and headed to the ladies' room. Halfway there, she retraced her steps and locked her office. No point making matters easier for the offender.

A short while later, after reapplying makeup and taking several paper towels to her shoes, Jackie emerged from the ladies' room with a sense of determination. Several of the secretaries were already seated at their desks, and she took a few extra moments to greet them. She even conversed with Melanie before returning to her office, not once mentioning the roses.

Now, standing in her own doorway, she felt emotionally drained and her legs threatened to give way. "Not by my strength," she whispered, and gently closed the door behind her.

Once all the rose petals had been heaped into a pile on her credenza, she sat at her desk and rang the vice president's office. Her hands no longer shook, and her heart had slowed to a normal pace.

"Hi, Carla, this is Jackie. Is Wilson back from lunch?"

"Yes, he is. Would you like to speak with him?"

"Yes, please."

Jackie looked up to see Melanie saunter by. Without thought, she smiled and waved at the blond woman.

"Hi, Jackie. What do you need?" Wilson asked pleasantly.

"As a matter of fact, I have some questions. May I come up?"

"Door's open."

Jackie replaced the phone and pulled a pad of paper and a pen from her desk. Not knowing how long she'd be in the vice president's office, she locked the door upon leaving.

One of the secretaries waved at her to get her attention.

"Jackie, I have the contract completed for tomorrow's closing," the pert brunette announced.

"Good," Jackie replied. "I'll stop by and get it on my way back from Wilson's office. By the way, Ginny, you look great in turquoise."

Ginny smiled. "Thanks. I'll have the papers on the corner of my desk."

Whirling around, Jackie nearly ran into Norm. "Excuse me."

He eyed her oddly and she felt a flicker of coldness before he cast his gaze upon the secretary. "Ginny," Norm began, "Melanie tells me she's having difficulty getting her contracts typed."

Ginny's green eyes widened and her face flushed. "That's not true, sir. I've done all her things as soon as she's given them to me."

"Melanie states otherwise."

Jackie had complete confidence in Ginny's professional performance. The years they had worked together indicated a competent employee. "Norm, perhaps there's been a mistake."

Norm Timmons clenched his jaw and faced Jackie. "I'll thank you to tend to your own business."

Jackie bit back a retort. A scene would not be wise, and she didn't know the details of Melanie's problem with the secretary. "I'm sorry," she replied. "Ginny has always been very efficient, that's all." Giving the secretary a reassuring smile, she walked toward the stairway.

Although Norm's handling of the matter with Ginny made her bristle, Jackie decided to look into it after her conversation with Wilson. One more item of contention to frustrate her, but not too much for God.

Entering his office, Wilson greeted her warmly. "This has to be good news," he said. "Locks are changed and our problem person can't possibly do any more dirty work."

She started to sit but changed her mind. "May I shut the door?"

"Certainly." The lines on his forehead deepened.

Once assured of privacy, she seated herself. "I don't know quite how to say this."

"Simply tell me what's going on." Wilson sighed.

Jackie nibbled on her lip, then repeated her findings. "I've been wondering, who else has a master key?"

"The cleaning crew."

"But they aren't in the building during the day."

"And you're sure the door was locked when you left?"

"Oh, yes." She pondered the situation while he, too, sat in obvious thought. "When did you get the key from the locksmith?"

"I didn't," he replied slowly. "Once I returned from lunch that day, Carla handed it to me."

"So the serviceman left it with her?" Jackie wouldn't give up until she solved her dilemma.

"I assume he did." Wilson picked up his phone and buzzed Carla. "Say, do you remember what time the locksmith finished last week and dropped off the master key with you?" Jackie studied the picture of Wilson Anderson's sweet family while Carla replied. "Hmm. Okay, thanks." Replacing the receiver, he glanced up at Jackie. "I don't see any indication of foul play. Carla was at lunch from twelve-thirty to one-thirty; and when she got back, Melanie brought her the key."

Jackie mentally calculated the time. She'd been gone from twelve to one to meet Reed, and during that hour the locksmith had arrived and completed his work. Melanie worked during her lunch; she was in the building before Jackie left and when she returned.

"So, I really think your office must have been unlocked today, which invited someone inside." He paused. "Jackie, I'm really sorry about your flowers. Are you sure you haven't made an enemy? Have you told me everything?"

She nodded, realizing that explaining the situation about Melanie and Reed would be foolhardy at this point. Wilson needed proof of foul play and so did Jackie. "Yes, I am at a loss about this. Seems to be one nasty deed after another."

The vice president stood and raked his fingers through his

hair. "At least we know now you are the one being targeted and not Melanie. I'd hate to lose a good employee over this." He shook his head. "That didn't sound right. I meant she's new to the bank, and these incidents could sway her to seek employment elsewhere. And you have been here long enough to endure the problems until we determine who's at fault."

Jackie agreed. "I'm ready for it to end right now."

"Don't blame you. So am I." He whirled around to his computer. "Think I'll check my calendar and clear some time for a staff meeting. All the employees should be reminded of the consequences involved here. Believe me, when I finally get the matter resolved, our troublemaker will be out of a job and facing possible felony charges."

Jackie hesitated. "I'm looking at the situation in two ways. One part of me believes the other employees might deter the offender and scare him or her off. The other wonders if the attention might make matters worse."

"You have an excellent point, but I'd like to have some good folks looking out for you. I'll schedule a meeting right away."

As she left Wilson's office, Jackie hoped having others be aware of the recent activity might solve the problem. He'd assured her that he wouldn't mention any names—only make the employees aware of the consequences of stealing or destroying personal and company property.

A peculiar tingling settled unexpectedly at the nape of her neck. Why did she suddenly doubt Wilson's tactics would end the problem?

Back in her office, Jackie's phone blinked with a message. Checking her voice mail, she learned Reed had called.

Swallowing hard, she returned his call. How could she tell him what happened?

"Hi, sunshine," he greeted, and she smiled sadly at the sound of his voice. "Got your E-mail and I'm glad you're enjoying the flowers. Very nicely worded, too."

"Good," she replied softly. "I meant every word of it. How is your day?"

"Oh," he chuckled, "educational, profitable, harried. What about yours?"

"Interesting."

"Do I detect a problem?"

She sighed. "Seems like I go from one crisis to another these days."

"I want to hear all about it." He sounded worried, and she detested telling him about the flowers.

"It's not pleasant."

"Most crises aren't."

She hesitated. "I hate telling you this, but while I dashed out for a hamburger at lunch, someone got into my locked office and cut the blooms off every one of your roses."

The silence hung in the air like a wretched stench.

"Melanie," he finally uttered, anger creeping through his low words.

"I thought of her, too," Jackie admitted. "And I want to talk to you about it more. . .in person."

"I can be at your apartment by six-thirty," he quickly said.

"All right. I'll talk to you then."

With the conversation finished, Jackie elected to talk to Ginny, but the woman had gone home for the day. The secretary who worked beside her reported Ginny had been extremely upset.

Why am I not surprised? Jackie asked herself, feeling a knot twist in her stomach. *How much more can go wrong?*

&

Pacing across the floor of his office, Reed battled his emotions. He slammed his fist into an open palm, not once but several times. Anger surged through his veins like liquid fire. He could handle Melanie hurting him, but not his Jackie. He wanted to call her and order her to lay off, except it would most likely incite more problems. That's how Melanie worked. Once she sunk her teeth into your skin, she didn't ease off until your flesh lay in shreds.

Melanie didn't want Reed back, but neither did she want him involved in a relationship with another woman. She'd prefer to see him made miserable by losing Jackie. How well he remembered her incessant need to be in control.

Reed realized destroying the roses was Melanie's trademark—her style, her vengeance, her evil ways. She knew he'd remember another identical performance from years before. Back then he'd felt more devastated than the flowers she mutilated. Now, he'd like to wring her neck.

Slow down, buddy. Give your frustration and fury to the One who can take care of it. Remember, this is not against flesh and blood; it's spiritual warfare, and the war is already won. Melanie doesn't know the Lord, and she is acting like a rebellious child. The Lord loves her the same as He does you.

Don't let anger rule your heart. Have pity on Melanie; seek out help for her, but most of all, love her through Jesus' eyes.

Reed walked to the window and stared out his glass wall. In the distance he viewed an azure afternoon sky slowly turning shades of gray as storm clouds gathered and rolled. As they tossed about, the sun peeked from behind and cast a brilliant light to earth, reminding him that it had been there all along. Just like God's love.

All right, Lord, he prayed, resigning himself to obedience. *I'll do what You ask.*

Pulling open a desk drawer, he secured a telephone directory. He searched through the resident pages until he found the name of Harold Copeland.

They aren't dead, he had told Jackie, *but alive and well. . . and praying every day for their lost daughter.*

sixteen

The doorbell of Jackie's apartment rang at precisely six-thirty. She wiped her hands on a towel in the kitchen where she'd been busy preparing supper.

"Who's there?" she asked, hurrying to the door.

"Your friendly delivery boy," Reed replied.

"Right." She unlatched the dead bolt, opened the door, and then stood frozen as Reed presented her with an open box of a dozen, long-stemmed roses, identical to the ones she'd received earlier in the day. "Oh, Reed," she murmured, flashing an appreciative gaze into his soft brown eyes, "you shouldn't be so extravagant."

"What's money when a beautiful woman is involved?" He grinned. "I'm told flowers are meant to last longer than a few hours."

She tilted her head and gave him a sad smile. "Normally they do, and these are more beautiful than the ones you sent this morning." Gathering up the box, she continued, "Please come in." As always, he looked magnificent.

Jackie closed the door behind him and noticed he seemed nervous. Instantly, she realized he hadn't been inside her apartment before, only at the door. The setting invited temptation, and he probably felt tense being alone with her. In the past, when he'd picked her up and brought her home, they'd said their hellos and good-byes at the door. She smiled, grateful for his strong morals. She carefully laid the box of flowers on the table, then turned to wrap her arms around his neck.

"You are wonderful. Thank you so much for the beautiful roses, both sets of them."

His arms slipped about her waist and he kissed her tenderly. "I'm sorry about today," he said and pulled her close.

"Well, I just forgot about it." Peering up into his eyes, she saw a reflection of herself.

Reed smiled and kissed her again, this time gently claiming her lips. With a sigh, he released her. "You are addictive," he claimed. "Much more, and you'll have to ask me to leave."

Sensing her own rising emotions, Jackie stepped back. "I'd better put these in water."

While Jackie arranged the flowers at the kitchen table, he stood and watched. "You can sit down," she offered, snipping a longer stem before inserting it into a vase.

"I will, when you finish."

Glancing up, she caught his eye. "I was in the mood to cook—a way to get rid of today's frustrations. Do you like chicken Alfredo?"

"Hmm, you bet. Can I help?"

"Probably," she said, sticking baby's breath in among the roses. "How are you at salads?"

He touched the back of her waist, sending a delicious tingle up her spine. "Just call me Chef Reed. I haven't lived all these years by myself and not whipped up a gourmet dish at a moment's notice."

She laughed at his admission. "You'll have to show me sometime."

"I'd love to," he replied. "But I warn you, my idea of gourmet may not be the same as yours."

"Such as?"

"Carryout served on real plates with real silverware and real glasses."

She ceased arranging the roses and gave him an unflinching gaze. "Now that has the chef's touch."

Laughing, the two prepared dinner. Jackie cooked the chicken Alfredo and buttered garlic bread, and Reed tossed a salad. They joked and teased, stealing quick kisses at opportune moments.

"What's for dessert?" Reed asked, pouring water through an ice tea maker.

Jackie hesitated. "I have some frozen chocolate chip cookie dough."

"Fantastic, my favorite." He licked his lips. He opened the freezer compartment of her refrigerator. "In here?"

"Yeah, top shelf, left-hand side." She cringed. "Reed?"

He whirled and offered a questioning look. "Yes."

She sighed. "The package may look a little strange. Sometimes I eat just plain cookie dough."

He chuckled and shook his head. "Thanks for warning me. Do you mind parting with a little for the real thing?"

Jackie swatted him with a towel. "Now, I make the one great confession of my soul and you harass me."

"Oh, no, sweetheart. I wouldn't dream of it. Your confession proves one thing, though. The next time I want to impress you, I'll simply mix up a batch of cookie dough."

She wagged her finger at him then feigned seriousness. "You know, it probably would work."

All through dessert, their merriment continued. Jackie knew the time would come when they'd need to discuss the day, but she hated to mention it. The evening had been perfect, too perfect to spoil it with an unpleasant topic.

Once they finished the last chocolate chip cookie, which Jackie swore was the best she'd ever eaten—baked or otherwise—the two began to clear the table.

"We do need to talk," he stated slowly, setting the butter and cheese inside the fridge.

"I know," she said reluctantly, avoiding his gaze. "Do you want to wait until we've cleaned up?"

"Sure. Tonight's been fun, hasn't it?"

"Yes. Maybe we could cook dinner together more often."

He kissed the tip of her nose. "Anytime." His lips tempted her, and as if perceiving her thoughts, he left a trail of kisses across her forehead, down her cheek, to her waiting mouth. Slipping his arms around her waist, he pulled her against his body.

"We need to stop," she urged, feeling her senses giving rise to passion.

"I agree," he said hoarsely, his eyes soft. "Perhaps we could take a walk while we discuss our little problem."

"Good idea." She nervously wiped off the kitchen table, laughing lightly. "I think I need to retract an earlier statement about us spending more evenings alone cooking dinner. It's probably too dangerous."

"Definitely dangerous. We probably should limit 'inside the apartment' time to ten minutes max."

A short while later, Jackie and Reed strolled hand in hand through the grounds of the apartment complex. The memory of his earlier kisses still left her breathless, especially with the scent of his cologne lingering on her blouse collar. They couldn't be alone again in her apartment or his for very long. It was simply too tempting. God wanted them pure, and the blessings of obedience far outweighed the consequences of sin.

Finally Reed asked the inevitable question. "Will you tell me about today? I want to hear every detail." He squeezed her hand lightly, silently encouraging her.

"Okay," she said, and repeated what happened with the roses and her later conversation with Wilson.

Reed listened until she finished. "I agree that alerting the other employees to what's going on is a good idea. At least, it should slow down Melanie."

"But why are you so sure she's at the bottom of this?" Jackie asked curiously.

He exhaled and fixed his gaze straight ahead. "Melanie has done this before. . .to me. She knew I'd remember."

Jackie shook her head in disbelief. "Why? What is the point of hurting you and me? I wonder at times if she's still in love with you."

"No, not at all," Reed quickly responded. "Melanie doesn't comprehend the meaning of love. I think when she was younger, she may have been in love with love, but now I think that's gone, too. Unfortunately, I think you and I are a game to her, something to keep her mind occupied." He paused and looked directly into Jackie's face. "What do you think about today?"

Uncertain how to express her true feelings, Jackie paused. "I really believe Melanie could have taken the master key and copied it before I returned from lunch last week. It's entirely possible she destroyed the roses, too. Oh, Reed. I hate the thought of accusing her."

"I understand," he said softly. "But we've got to find a way to bring this to an end. She needs to be caught before some-one else gets hurt. Has anything else happened?"

She pondered his question, then remembered the incident with Norm and Ginny. After relaying that conversation, Jackie added, "Ginny has always been a dependable employee. I find it hard to believe Melanie's accusation. Of course, I don't know the entire story either."

He appeared to be deep in thought, and Jackie decided not to question him. She'd reached the point of not wanting to think or talk about Melanie's capabilities.

Finally he chose to speak. "Tell me about Norm Timmons. What kind of guy is he?"

Jackie swallowed, carefully selecting her words. "Well. . . you already know he's the head of the loan department, both commercial and real estate. He's unsaved, enjoys parties, is single, and he admires Melanie."

"No need to say more. I have the picture," Reed said dryly. He tugged on her hand, and when she turned toward him, he planted a kiss on her cheek.

"Do you think she's feeding him lies about Ginny?" she inquired curiously.

He shrugged. "Probably, and if he's hearing things about her, chances are you're in the middle of it, too."

"Wonderful. I'm not his favorite person."

"Then she has allied herself with a man who will sympa-thize with her." A frown creased his handsome face. "I did phone Melanie's parents today and talked to Mr. Copeland. Guess she broke off relations with them about seven years ago. I decided to tell him where she's working."

"Do you think they'll contact her?"

He shook his head. "Her father said he and his wife felt they should honor her request that they stay away from her. He went on to ask me if she had gotten into trouble."

Jackie sensed a churning in her stomach. "And what did you tell him?"

His face looked grim. "I purposely sounded vague—told him she hadn't at this point, but her actions were not leading in a good direction. He asked me to stay in touch."

"Oh, those poor people," Jackie murmured. "And to think she wanted me to believe they were deceased."

"I feel sorry for them, too. Mr. Copeland sounded so tired, said he'd lived with Melanie's problems for a lifetime. She really needs help, before it's too late."

Frustration needled Jackie. "What will it take to stop her?"

He shrugged his shoulders, and they paused in their walk. "Eight years ago, with me, she got tired of the charade."

Jackie saw the tiny lines around his eyes. Things like this didn't happen to real people, only in books and movies. Suddenly she felt selfish. "I'm sorry, Reed. I'm so wound up in myself that I fail to see what Melanie's tricks are doing to you."

He gave her a reassuring smile. "I'm fine; my main concern is you. But—well, I wanted to ask you. . ."

"About what?" she asked.

"Can we pray for her when we get back to your apartment?" He stood still on the sidewalk and faced her squarely. "I don't want you to think I have any feelings for Melanie. Truth is, I'm trying not to condemn her; instead, I need to see her through the eyes of Jesus." He swallowed hard. "This afternoon I felt so full of hate and revenge. God had to do some heavy-duty work on me. One thing He showed me is she's disturbed and ill—besides being a sinner and headed toward a dead end if someone doesn't get through to her soon."

Jackie felt her heart beating rapidly. At first she had feared Reed still cared for Melanie, but the look in his eyes told her otherwise. This man before her had obviously been victimized many times by Melanie's pranks. Yet, he loved God above all things. It would be too easy for Reed and Jackie to despise her, but praying for Melanie brought her needs into focus—where she might allow God to touch and heal her.

"I think you have a wonderful idea," she replied, lifting her chin.

"Thank you, but it originated from God. I know what I'm asking isn't easy, but I believe it's the only way to handle the problems and glorify Him, too."

Once back at the apartment, she suggested Reed check his phone messages at home. Jackie suspected Melanie might have called him, and he might not tell her about it otherwise. Studying his face while he listened to his calls nearly broke her heart. Without asking, Jackie knew Melanie had phoned.

"I want to hear the message," she whispered, peering into his troubled face. "Please, don't keep anything from me. We're in this together."

"This firms up all we talked about tonight," he said. "It's not the kind of thing I want to share with you."

"I don't care. I need to understand what we're fighting."

Reluctantly he nodded, punched a few more buttons on the phone, and handed it to Jackie.

"Hi, Reed. I saw the roses you sent Jackie today. They were lovely—too lovely for Miss Goody-goody. She didn't deserve them, and I wanted them for myself. I really couldn't help myself. My darling, when are you going to realize how much I still love you? I want you back, and I'll do anything to make sure we are together again."

Much later, long after Reed had gone home, Jackie lay in bed and mulled over the situation with Melanie. She couldn't begin to imagine life without the Lord. No purpose. No direction. No unconditional love and hope for eternal life. Reed had been right. Melanie needed their prayers above all else. That evening, she and Reed had taken turns lifting Melanie to their heavenly Father, praying for her salvation and release from the depravity raging her soul.

Moments before she fell asleep, Jackie realized she and Reed could not share a future until the circumstances surrounding Melanie were laid to rest.

Can I endure it all? she asked herself. *Is the relationship with Reed worth not knowing what will happen next?* Jackie knew she loved him, but thinking about the fight ahead made her weary.

ᵃ

Two days later, Melanie sat in her office, biting back her anger at Wilson Anderson's impromptu meeting. So Miss Goody-goody took her little hurt feelings to the big boss. How special. Now all the employees would be spying on each other. Melanie had always been careful, but now she'd have to come up with different tactics.

Hmm. She tapped her finger against her cheek. Wilson's proclamation might be to her advantage. If nothing happened for three or four weeks, Jackie would get comfortable. *She might think it's all over, relax, and believe her God has answered her prayers.*

She has to realize it's me, Melanie thought with a satisfied smile. *If not, she's more stupid than I ever thought. Of course, if she mentioned the beheaded roses, Reed would remember another similar incident.*

Melanie stood to contain her excitement. She recalled the many times she'd schemed and won in the past. Men were such idiots, and she had eagerly lured the wealthy and powerful ones into her clutches, then upped the stakes. Simple strategy, but it worked; her bank account proved how men would pay anything to save their reputations.

Some affairs were more pleasant than others, and some brought in more money. The last liaison in Chicago nearly cost her job. Luckily, the position became open in Toledo when it did, or she'd been out of work and possibly facing legal charges.

Oh, but she loved the excitement.

With a little giggle, she anticipated the future. When Melanie finished with Jackie, she'd hand over dear Reed on a golden platter. But just as before, Melanie planned to discard him like three-day-old garbage. She had her sights on better things—Wilson Anderson.

seventeen

Three weeks later, Reed visited his land to inspect the stakes where the construction crew had marked the perimeters for his basement. Tomorrow, the contractor and his construction crew planned to start digging. For months, Reed had envisioned the two-story structure in its various stages of construction, and this marked the beginning. Excitement nudged at him as he imagined his and Jackie's new home.

Pulling a digital camera from his pocket, Reed snapped four pictures, one from each direction. He chuckled, realizing no one else would ever value his detailed scrapbook of a start-to-finish building project. But when he'd fostered the idea of designing his own home years ago and finally sketched it on paper, it seemed natural to record every inch of its progress. Now, he thought of little else except sharing his dream with Jackie.

He'd consulted her about the smallest of details, making certain she approved of the interior and exterior features. She'd been a trooper at helping him make selections by gathering magazine and newspaper articles with pictures regarding the latest decorating trends. He'd researched ways to build the best house but hadn't given much thought to wood stains and kitchen cabinets. The two spent many hours driving through newly established neighborhoods and studying model homes before he made a decision.

Reed had to laugh at the way Jackie took careful note of his preferences. When he mentioned he liked straight simple lines, she suggested visiting builders' showrooms for contemporary styling. Everything from the design of exterior lighting fixtures to the type of hardwood floors and interior lighting required careful thought. Fortunately, they shared similar tastes and ideas, which pleased Reed even more.

"Come on, Yukon," he called to his pet. "We need to go." Immediately the dog perked up his furry head and raced toward him.

They'd be back on Saturday, this time with Jackie. Strange, before Reed met her, he'd been perfectly content by himself—and with his dog. These days, he felt lonely and unfulfilled without her. Glancing down at Yukon, he patted the dog affectionately.

Hmm, man's best friend, he thought with a smile. *That is, until God brings a woman into a man's life.*

Soon Reed traveled back to Toledo, his mind spinning with thoughts of Jackie and their future.

The past three weeks had sped by with no problems from Melanie. Reed wanted to believe she'd taken Wilson Anderson's advice and ceased the underhanded activity. In fact, he'd thanked God for the peace. Nothing angered him more than Melanie attempting to sabotage Jackie's professional and personal life. He'd stopped trying to figure out Melanie's motives, because all of the causes pointed to the same thing—Melanie did not have a relationship with Jesus Christ. She behaved like a nonbeliever, a person overcome with greed and control. And just like the elder Copelands and Jackie, Reed prayed for her salvation.

Dusk had settled as he drove back into Toledo. He punched in Jackie's number from his phone, but she didn't answer. When her cell phone was busy, he left a voice mail message. Odd, Jackie thought she'd be home from Shanna's by now. He knew the sisters had shared dinner while Jeff worked late. Shanna's due date had come and gone, leaving the entire family full of expectation about the baby's birth.

Easing his Blazer into the left lane, Reed switched on the radio to a Mud Hens game in the top of the ninth inning. He waited a few minutes in his driveway until the baseball team won.

Once inside his apartment, he noticed his answering machine flashing. Certain it was from Jackie, he quickly pressed the play button.

"Hi, Reed. I'm at Toledo Hospital. Shanna's water broke while we were having dinner, so I called Jeff and he met us at the hospital. Her contractions started right away at five minutes apart. Whew! Scared me to death! I thought I might have to deliver her baby! Jeff is with Shanna now, and Mom and Dad are on their way. If you want, you could come, too. I now have my cell phone on, so give me a call."

He grinned and snatched up his wallet, cell phone, and keys. *A new baby,* he thought appreciatively. *I'd like a whole house full of those.* Breathing a prayer for Shanna and the baby's health, he hurried back to his Blazer.

Shortly thereafter, Reed found Jackie and her parents seated in the maternity ward's waiting room. Ron and Nita had chosen a teal-colored vinyl sofa while Jackie relaxed in a matching chair.

"Jeff's with Shanna," Jackie explained after he'd greeted them. Her hazel eyes were wide with expectation. "She wants only him in the delivery room with her. According to Jeff, it won't be long before he's a daddy."

"I never asked, is it a boy or girl?" Reed asked.

Jackie shrugged. "Neither of them wanted to know ahead of time. Guess it will be a surprise to all of us."

Nita Mason shook her snow-white head, obviously miffed. "They wouldn't even share any names with us. Imagine that? I'm about to receive my first grandchild and have no idea what little he or she will be called."

Ron held his wife's hand. "Now, honey, Shanna and Jeff want it all to be a surprise package."

"I know," Nita replied, her voice softening, "and I'm sorry. Looks like I'm being a mom, worrying about my little girl and complaining about silly things."

Sensing the tension of the waiting game and the distinct possibility of being at the hospital for hours, Reed's stomach reminded him of its need for dinner. "Why don't I go get us some sandwiches and coffee?"

"Sounds like a wonderful idea," Jackie replied. "Would you like some company? I can't hurry this baby by sitting here."

Reed reached to pull her to her feet and clasped her hand firmly in his. Their eyes met briefly, yet long enough for Jackie to blush. He grinned, loving the effect he had on her.

After Ron and Nita gave them their food orders, Reed and Jackie left for the cafeteria.

"I am not particularly fond of hospital food," she whispered in the elevator. "It's always a toss between deluxe cardboard and flavorless."

He planted a kiss on her cheek. "I agree, except it's gotten me alone with you."

"You're totally undisciplined," she accused, a smile playing on her upturned lips. "But I'm glad you're here. Jeff was a blubbery mess when he arrived at the hospital. He's so sensitive, Reed, and he must have thanked me a hundred times for bringing Shanna tonight."

"I think I'd have to be on medication if I were in his shoes." Reed chuckled. "You know, your brothers and sisters are pretty lucky having you as a big sis."

Jackie shook her head as though denying his words. "I believe it's the other way around, but thanks."

Reed watched the elevator numbers slowly descend to level two, the site of the cafeteria. Suddenly he remembered the handicaps of the other Mason children. "Are the older boys looking out for the younger ones tonight?"

She shook her head. "No. Mom and Dad have a nursing service on call for times like tonight when neither of them can be at home."

"Good idea. Paul doing all right?" The elevator door opened, and the two stepped out into a blue gray hallway.

"Yes, quite good actually. He really admires you. Until you came into the picture, Paul claimed he was at a disadvantage because he's black and adopted by white parents. Now, he feels God has placed him within our family for a reason."

"And he's content?" Reed questioned, his interest kindled.

"He says so."

Before sharing his thoughts, Reed considered the young man's struggle with growing up and racial issues. "I'd like to spend some time alone with him, if that's okay with your parents. You see, my position at his age ranged between total rebellion and anger. Because I had one black biological parent and one white, I felt as though I didn't belong anywhere."

Jackie tilted her head and peered up into his face, dark brown curls spilling over her shoulders. "So it all changed when you gave your life to the Lord?"

"Not exactly. I got saved in junior high, but not until after the mess with Melanie did I fully understand how God looks at a person's heart, not the color of his skin."

Reed saw Jackie's eyes soften and moisten with emotion. "I'm sorry you had to experience a broken heart to realize God's love for you."

He smiled and his thumb lightly brushed a tear rolling down her cheek. "I'm not sorry. Our Lord used those days to make me strong in Him. What I considered a weakness, a flaw in me, God intended for good. That's what I want to share with Paul."

She took a deep breath. "I am so lucky to have you as a friend. . .so lucky."

"So now do you understand why it doesn't matter to me about your ethnic background?" Reed squeezed her hand. "Oh, I definitely think you are the most gorgeous woman alive, but it's your heart I love."

Jackie's hazel gaze widened in surprise.

He grimaced and shook his head. "I'm such an idiot. I didn't plan to tell you I love you in a hospital corridor."

She lifted her chin and fairly beamed. "Seems like the perfect place to me. And. . ." The two now stood outside the double doors leading into the cafeteria. "I'm honored, pleased, tickled, happy, and I love you, too."

Reed pulled her to the side of the hallway. With no one in sight, he kissed her tenderly. "We have tons of things to talk about," he whispered, "after Shanna and Jeff's baby is born."

As the two waited in line to order sandwiches, Reed's mind sped over Jackie's declaration of love for him. He found it nearly impossible to concentrate on the food orders, and Jackie must have felt the same, for they had a difficult time remembering what Ron and Nita wanted.

Reed couldn't remember feeling so incredibly happy. Fighting the urge to wrap his arms around his beloved, his words stumbled as he selected potato chips and pretzels. When he spilled the coffee and struggled through a futile attempt at snapping plastic lids on the hot cups, Jackie burst into laughter.

"You're nervous," she giggled, giving him a hand.

. He feigned a disapproving look. "And it's all your fault."

Shaking like a teenage boy who just asked out the prom queen, he returned her laughter. This must be something else love did to a person.

A few moments later, Reed and Jackie exited the elevator and walked back into the waiting room, armed with sandwiches, chips, coffee, and a half-dozen chocolate chip cookies. As soon as Reed saw Ron and Nita's faces, he sensed something had gone terribly wrong. Instantly, all their excitement dissipated. He set the food down on an end table and took the coffee from Jackie.

"What is it?" she asked, her voice quivering. She glanced from one parent to the other.

"The doctor has decided to do a Caesarean section," Ron replied gravely, through narrowed, gray eyes.

Startled, Jackie blurted out, "But I thought everything looked great and she'd deliver soon."

"Apparently not," Ron explained, reaching for his wife's hand. "But this procedure is common, and Jeff has complete confidence in her doctor's ability. We simply need to continue praying for Shanna and the baby."

"We've phoned the children to pray, too," Nita said with an encouraging smile. "Would you two like to join us?"

The four held hands and Ron prayed, "Heavenly Father, we come before You praising Your name and Your mighty works. We know You are in control of all things, and this isn't a surprise to You. At times like these, I can't help but feel like David who asked 'what is man that You are mindful of him. . .that You care for him?' We know You love Shanna, Jeff, and their baby, and we know they are in Your care. We are trusting them to You, Lord. Give the doctor wisdom and guide his hands through the delivery of this little one. In Jesus' name, amen."

Reed marveled at the strength evident in Ron Mason's faith. The tall, thin man reminded him so much of his own father—strong, tender, and trusting. Both men worked hard at imitating Jesus. Reed deeply desired to someday lead his own household in the direction of God's provision. Glancing at Jackie, he realized they had been put together as a part of the Father's wondrous plan.

A feeling of peace washed over him. Whatever happened, he knew Shanna and the baby were safe in God's hands.

eighteen

Shortly before midnight, Jeffery Blake Robertson II entered the world with a loud cry, weighing in at eight pounds, eleven ounces. Shanna and her infant son waltzed through the birth with no further complications—although Jeff became slightly ill and nearly fainted when he learned about the Caesarean.

Jackie cried with relief and joy, as did her mother, and her father let out a hearty "praise God" that roared over the entire maternity ward. He hugged his wife and the others before rushing to the nearest phone to call his other children.

An hour later, Jackie, Reed, Jeff, and the elated grandparents peered at the baby through the glass wall of the nursery. Shanna needed her rest, so the group had whispered their good nights and decided to pay a visit to the tiniest member of the family.

"He looks like Shanna," Jeff pointed out, jamming his hands in his pants pockets and teetering on his heels.

Jackie studied the infant's face, all wrinkled and puckered. "I reserve passing judgment just yet. My sister doesn't really look like this baby, except for the eyes."

The proud grandpa enjoyed a laugh. "So are we to call him Jeff?"

The new father shook his head and stared admiringly at his son. "No, we want to call him Blake. He needs his own identity."

Nita, still filled with emotion, sighed and dabbed her eyes. "It's a beautiful name for a beautiful baby boy. I'm so happy." She sniffed quite loudly, which prompted the rest of them to share another laugh.

Jackie snuggled against Reed's side while observing her nephew. "I could watch him the rest of the night, but unfortunately, we have to work tomorrow."

"Yeah. It will come earlier than we'd like," Reed agreed. "But he is wonderful. I bet we'll be given lots of opportunities to baby-sit." He tapped lightly on the glass as though Blake would give him full attention. "Hey, little one, now that you are here, what do you think of this world?" As if on cue, the baby opened his mouth wide and let out a howl. "Oops, looks like I asked the wrong question."

Jackie giggled. "Must be your timing. This is all new to him."

"And me," Jeff added, his face flushed with the excitement. He pressed his face closer to the glass. "I think he has a pitcher's arm. Look at the way he throws it back and forth."

"You're wrong," Jackie insisted, lightly jabbing her brother-in-law in the ribs. "Blake has a music conductor's arm."

Jeff pretended to ignore her, but he couldn't stop his grin spreading from ear to ear.

Shortly thereafter, in the parking lot, Jackie lingered over good-byes with Reed. As they leaned against her Camaro, their arms wrapped around each other's waist, she wanted the night to last forever. Now, since they had confessed their love, she wanted to talk, cuddle, stroll in the moonlight, and share sweet kisses under the stars.

"I really do need to go," she finally admitted, resting her head upon his shoulder. "It's already morning."

"Yes, but I'd be content holding you until the sun comes up." He kissed her forehead. "You're standing by a very selfish man."

"We'll act like zombies at work," she pointed out.

"True."

"Probably be cranky and have horrible headaches."

"For sure." Reed chuckled.

"But I don't really care."

"Well, one of us has to be strong, and it looks like it has to be me." Reed stepped back and opened her car door with a chivalric gesture for her to get inside. "You'd better hurry and slide in before I lose my resolve," he added.

Jackie laughed. "Okay, I'm going." She settled onto the soft gray leather, and they exchanged one more light kiss before she stuck her key into the ignition.

"I love you," he whispered. "And I'll call you later at work."

She smiled and nodded. "I love you, too." Jackie felt nothing could ever possibly separate them now. They'd weathered the weeks of Melanie's tricks, but now those days were gone—her coworker had obviously given up on getting him back. Dazzled by the evening's events, she blew him a kiss and drove home.

❧

Listening to the rain pelt against the window in her office only made Melanie's mood sink deeper. She'd been fighting depression for the last several days, and although she should be accustomed to the demon, it always took her by surprise. Like a curse or an evil spell, Melanie termed the melancholia her mystic monster. It forced her to paint on a facade of vivacity, when in reality she felt despondent and paralyzed.

Melanie lacked a diversion, a project or activity to push her mind free of the gloom. She didn't carry drugs in her purse, neither the prescribed nor illegal ones—just in case someone ever questioned her sanity. But she had them at home for emergencies. She was considering taking something as soon as she got home from work when Jackie walked by.

What could Reed possibly see in her? Melanie silently seethed. Oh, she would look all right, if she'd shorten those skirts and wear more makeup. But obviously Jackie didn't know how to have fun. Why, the lunches they shared were positively boring. To make matters worse, Melanie had to consider every word before she spoke it, playing the role of the good girl. She watched the olive-skinned young woman stop to chat with a secretary; laughing, glowing, deliriously happy. Melanie wondered if her good spirits came from Reed or the nephew Melanie had heard was born the previous night.

Disgusting, Melanie inwardly criticized. *She should be at her desk working.* As the sound of Jackie's soft voice floated to her ears, Melanie clenched her fists; she loathed the way the others seemingly adored her. It took all Melanie's strength to fight the contempt searing her heart. Times like these, her carefully designed plans couldn't move fast enough. She wanted it all—now.

Besides dealing with Jackie, Melanie had to contend with Norm, the hedgehog. The man grated on her nerves, and when he touched her, she wanted to vomit. Unfortunately, she needed the repugnant man's help to carry out her schemes, which meant she boosted his ego no matter what the cost.

An idea began to dance across her mind, something to make the waiting worth every dreary second. In the past, she'd shed a few tears in Norm's presence, saying Jackie had mistreated her. Since he didn't care for Miss Goody-goody, he easily believed the fabrications. Norm had repeatedly asked if he could approach Jackie about the matter, but Melanie had refused. Maybe now was the right time for him to question Jackie's professional ethics. Given enough dramatics, Norm could even be persuaded to attach a discipline report to her file. If fed enough lies, he might bring it to Wilson's attention.

Grasping her planner, Melanie checked the date. *Yes,* she thought triumphantly. Enough time had passed to indulge in a little fun of her own. *The perfect cure for the monster.* This little pleasure-seeking venture should ease her restlessness and depression, she decided, reveling in what was yet to come.

೪

Two days later during the middle of the day, Jackie closed an auto loan for a father co-signing on his son's application. The young man had just graduated from college and had secured an excellent position with a computer company, but he didn't possess any credit. Luckily, his father opted to help him out.

Jackie rose from her chair and escorted the two men to the bank's lobby. As they passed the information counter, she selected information about Today's Bank checking and savings accounts and handed it to the younger man.

"With your new career and a new car, I invite you to start your banking with us," she suggested. "The pamphlet explains our many services and convenient hours."

After both men thanked her for all the work she'd done to secure the auto loan, she left them in the lobby and headed back to her office. Along the way, she met Norm exiting his office.

"Good afternoon," Jackie greeted pleasantly. "And how are you today?"

His gray eyes glared at her coldly. "I've been better. What are you doing?"

Taken by surprise, she gave her supervisor a small, questioning smile. "I'm going back to my office."

"Where have you been?"

Jackie dampened her lips. *Why the unnecessary questioning?* "I just closed an auto loan. While escorting them from my office, I gathered additional information for one of the customers."

He raised a bushy eyebrow, recently dyed to match his walnut-colored hairpiece. "Can we talk privately in my office?"

"Certainly." Jackie felt her heart pound as she heard the bitterness in his voice. Nothing about this conversation sounded pleasant, and she rummaged through her brain searching for an explanation.

After she had followed Norm into his steel-gray office, he closed the door behind him. He buttoned his navy blue sports jacket over his bulging stomach before sitting at his desk. "Jackie, I think this conversation is highly overdue," he began. "We have some serious problems between you and Melanie that need to be rectified as soon as possible."

Jackie felt her stomach roll—the same sick feeling she'd experienced just a few weeks ago. "I don't understand what you are talking about," she replied evenly. "Melanie and I have a good working relationship."

"In whose eyes?" he snapped. Leaning forward, his jacket button burst open. "Your denial of the shocking manner in which you have treated such a fine employee leaves me at a loss for words. The only reason I have not confronted you before this is she feared you would make her working environment even more difficult."

Lord, guide me through this, Jackie quickly prayed. "Would you explain what you are talking about?"

Norm Timmons's neck and face flushed crimson. He jerked open a desk drawer and pulled out a pad of paper where he'd already scribbled down something. Picking up the phone, he punched in a number and waited for a reply. "Melanie, could you step into my office for a few minutes?" He paused and nodded. "Thank you."

As if on cue, Melanie strolled in and seated herself. She crossed her legs, inching the already short skirt up her thighs. Jackie felt a wave of iciness swirl around the room and wrap its chill around her.

"Thank you for coming," Norm stated pleasantly to Melanie. "I wanted you present while I go over the problems between you and Jackie. This way you can answer any questions arising during the course of our conversation. For your information, Jackie states that she is unaware of any inappropriate treatment of you."

Melanie glanced down at her hands primly folded in her lap and reached for a tissue on his desk. He turned to Jackie with the notepad in front of him. "We will start at the beginning. Melanie tells me you refused to offer her any assistance or training when she first joined us. Even to this day, she is concerned her work performance may not be adequate."

"I believe she's mistaken," Jackie replied calmly. "I spent one full week with her and half days the following week. We discussed every facet of the real estate loan department, going over each current application and the policies of Today's Bank. I gave her a copy of everything we discussed, including the status of each customer's application. Melanie sat in on all the closings until she announced she could handle the procedures on her own. Even then I continued to attend closings to make sure she had all the paperwork in order."

"Excuse me," Melanie said, her voice dripping with sweetness. "Norm, I've already shared with you what happened during those first two weeks. On those training days, Jackie did very little except open the file drawers and show me where she kept everything. She distinctly said my experience at the Chicago branch should be sufficient. As far as a file filled with information to make my job easier. . .well, I never saw it. Regretfully, I must say Jackie insisted upon gossiping about the other employees, supplying me with inappropriate information about them."

Norm said nothing until he finished making notes. "What type of information?"

Melanie sighed and dabbed her eyes with the tissue. "Oh. . . who attended church. . .who had less than desirable personal lives. . ."

"That's simply not true," Jackie interrupted. "I'd like to see the proof of all your accusations."

Melanie immediately broke into sobs. The small office echoed with her cries as she repeatedly apologized for her display of emotion. Finally she gathered her composure. "I don't have any," she managed. "And everyone believes you're a saint and wouldn't ever do such horrible things."

Jackie stared pointedly into Melanie's tear-laden face. "Then give me one good reason why I would want you to perform badly. Remember, I was the one working overtime and weekends with both positions."

Melanie stiffened in her chair. "Reed Parker. You despise me because he and I were once engaged. It's jealousy." She turned to Norm. "I told you she'd deny it all. There's nothing I can do."

Jackie stood, committed to maintaining her professional countenance. "This is a ridiculous set of lies, and I'm not wasting any more of my time or the bank's by listening to it." She walked to the door, then whirled around and glanced from Melanie's ice blue gaze to Norm's narrow gray stare. "I have better things to do than conjure up stories about innocent people." As she reached for the knob, Melanie sobbed even harder.

"What about the E-mail you sent Wilson stating you weren't pleased with my work progress or the way I conducted myself around the other employees?" Melanie asked.

"I didn't do that either," Jackie replied, as she kept right on walking through the door. *Praise God,* she inwardly thought. *Thank You, Father.* Melanie had finally slipped. The only person who knew about the phony E-mail message was Wilson. But Jackie didn't see any reason to divulge that fact. If Melanie had elected to bring her tricks and lies to the surface, then let her think Jackie didn't have the intelligence to store ammunition.

nineteen

Once Jackie entered her office and settled into her chair, she took a deep breath. No one would ever see how the confrontation with Norm and Melanie had disturbed her. Never before had she been the target of such lies and devious schemes. Glancing at the gold-framed Scripture on her desk, she read: *I can do everything through him who gives me strength. Philippians 4:13.* She sighed as God's peace enveloped her.

Jackie believed Norm chose today to approach her since Wilson was on vacation for the week. Jackie couldn't take the matter to any other bank officers, because they didn't know the circumstances. It would all have to wait until Wilson returned and untangled the mess.

So Melanie had enlisted the support of Norm in her personal vendetta. Poor man. Jackie felt nothing but pity for him. Melanie had said some condescending things about him when the two women had gone to lunch, but Jackie couldn't prove that any more than Melanie could support her accusations. The idea of repeating gossip went against everything Jackie believed in.

Why did Melanie find it necessary to attack her? Jackie felt certain her coworker had become obsessed with controlling Reed. After all, she'd left the message on his answering machine stating how much she loved him. How long would it take before Melanie realized she couldn't manipulate people to her own purposes? Unfortunately, Norm Timmons had been mesmerized by her charm.

After work, Jackie drove straight home. Reed had arranged for them to see a movie, but she doubted if she could concentrate. Prayer had brought its share of comfort during the afternoon, but she desperately wanted to talk to him and feel his arms around her.

⮞

Reed unlocked his apartment and greeted Yukon, who was poised with the leash in his mouth, ready for a jaunt around the complex. Leaning his briefcase against a kitchen cabinet, Reed glanced at the answering machine flashing red with a recorded message.

"Hold on a minute," he said to the impatient dog. "Let me catch this call."

Pressing the play button, he bent to hug his pet until a familiar voice vied for his attention. "Hi, Reed. I bet you thought I'd given up on you. Well, I haven't. You slippery man, I'll have you yet." Melanie giggled and sighed seductively into the phone. "We did have our good times, now, didn't we? Don't you miss me? By the way, I do have news for you, that is if sweet Jackie hasn't already informed you about this afternoon. I suggest you kiss her good-bye before things become more unpleasant for her. Today was. . .well. . .traumatic, to say the least. And the plans I have for her future at Today's Bank get worse. It's up to you, Reed. Are you going to come back to me, or do I destroy your sweet girlfriend?" *Click.*

Slowly, he stood from his kneeling position. If he could only get rid of Melanie as easily as she'd disposed of him eight years before. Meanwhile, her words reverberated in his mind. He felt completely helpless and angry. Memories from the past pressed on him—the times Melanie insisted upon arguing about stupid things, then belittled him when he gave into her unending demands. Her laughter now echoed around him like evil omens. Control. It was her life's blood. Why couldn't she be stopped? And what had she done to Jackie?

Reed snatched up his cell phone, and with Yukon tugging on the leash, he called Jackie while he stepped outside to walk his pet.

"Jackie?"

"Hi."

Her voice sounded distant, and he longed to gaze into her hazel eyes and draw her into his arms. "What's going on?" he demanded, then immediately regretted his harsh tone.

"I'm sorry, honey. Our friend Melanie left a message on my machine indicating she'd made your day miserable."

"Oh, she did." Jackie tried to laugh.

"Why didn't you call me?" he asked, as gently as his concern allowed.

"I. . ." Jackie's voice faltered. "It seems like I'm always whining to you about something she's done. And we were going to see a movie tonight."

"Honey," he replied, torn between irritation and frustration, "you have never whined to me about anything. Forget the movie. Can I come over?"

She paused, and he envisioned her twisting a dark curl around her finger as she wrestled with indecision. "I would really like to see you, but we don't have to discuss today."

"Yes, we do. Give me a few minutes to walk the dog and I'll be over."

"Good. Will you tell me everything she said?"

She sounded weak, as though she'd been through a beating. He despised whatever Melanie had done to her. It had to stop! "No," he answered. "It's enough for you to know she's pleased with herself."

"All right." Jackie sighed. "I hope you change your mind before you get here."

"I won't. I'll see you soon, sweetheart."

Reed slipped the phone inside his pants pocket. Again anger threatened to rule his emotions; it oozed from his pores like infection from a festered wound. *Lord, God, help me,* he prayed. *It's wrong for Melanie to punish Jackie because of me! How can I stop her? What should I do?* Over and over he cried out for help until finally he felt the heat from his wrath diffuse. In his mind, he heard again the answer from the message Melanie had left. *It's up to you, Reed. Are you going to come back to me, or do I destroy your sweet girlfriend?* Reed closed his eyes and prayed for a clear answer. He refused to go back to Melanie—not for any reason, but he could break off the relationship with Jackie for her own protection.

The mere idea of not holding her again. . .not hearing her

melodious voice. . .the torture of separating from the one true love of his life seared his heart. Yet, if he truly loved Jackie, her well-being must come before his selfish desires. He must protect her from all the harm Melanie could conceivably inflict. His beloved deserved peace.

But Jackie read his heart like an artist perceives a picture. She would comprehend his motive and tell him nothing Melanie could do mattered. They loved each other and they belonged together; the obstacles weren't important. Perhaps not for Jackie, but Reed refused to tolerate it another day.

Thinking back over the past weeks, he'd seen the sorrow and disappointment in Jackie each time Melanie pulled another stunt. No more. With God as his strength, he planned to end it tonight.

Wearily, he plodded back to the apartment. Yukon must have sensed Reed's grief, for the dog brushed against his leg and peered into his master's face. Already feeling the pangs of loneliness and misery, Reed patted the animal's furry head. "After tonight, it's back to you and me, fella. I know you'll miss her, too."

After changing into jeans and a white pullover, he drove the familiar streets to Jackie's apartment. How he hated what must be done, but it had to be, for her sake! Promptly at seven o'clock, he stood at her door, still sorting out what to say. The mere sight of her made him ache. He wanted to remember exactly how she looked tonight—her dark curls pulled back from her face and cascading down her back, the hint of blush to her cheeks when she saw him, and most importantly, the sparkle of life and love in her eyes. She wore his favorite color, a royal blue shirt tucked inside slim-fitting jeans. He'd remember these moments forever.

"Come in," Jackie whispered, her gaze meeting his.

He wanted to kiss her lips, feel their softness and warmth, but he couldn't. It wasn't fair to her. . .or him. "I hurried over," Reed said, wishing he'd devised more clever words.

"I'm really all right. I'm made of stronger stuff than Melanie can dish out. Would you like something to drink?"

"Water is fine," he replied, wondering if asking for water took advantage of her. After all, he'd come to end their relationship.

She stepped into the kitchen, and he seated himself on a kitchen chair. Sitting on her white leather sofa seemed dangerous. He could easily give into the temptation of kissing away his purpose.

"What's wrong?" She handed him the water.

Before taking a sip, he noted the concerned look on her face. "Just worried about you. Please, tell me what happened."

Jackie slipped into a chair across from him and relayed the afternoon's events. All the while, Melanie's ultimatum screamed in his thoughts.

"She doesn't give up," he finally stated. "The problems at the bank will steadily get worse."

"But her accusations can't be proven," Jackie reasoned.

"It threatens your reputation and credibility."

"Wilson will clear things up, and now that I know for sure she sent the E-mail to him, he can question her further. It's simply a matter of time."

Reed nodded slowly, acknowledging her explanation. He had to get this over with. Slowly he stood and stared briefly at the glass. He hadn't taken a drink of the water. "I've been thinking," he began, avoiding her hazel eyes. "This relationship isn't working out like I'd planned. The problems with Melanie have affected my work, and I can't have a woman threatening my career. So, I'm calling it quits between us." He swallowed hard and his mouth grew dry. "You're a beautiful woman, Jackie, and I'm honored to have known you, but I can't deal with Melanie and her threats against you anymore."

He walked toward the door, thinking once he made it to the Blazer, the nightmare would all be behind him. Like a movie in slow motion, his hand couldn't get to the knob fast enough. Once there, he turned for a brief moment—one last time to feast on her delicate features. "I'm sorry." He walked away from the only woman he'd ever truly loved.

With trembling legs, Jackie clenched the sides of a ladder-back chair in an effort to keep from crumbling to the floor. Crushed beyond imagination, she stood in the pit of hopelessness. His words had paralyzed her senses and rendered her body helpless and quivering. A wave of sickness swept over her as she stared at the door. Soon, he'd knock and she'd find these last few shocking minutes were nothing but a bad dream. The longer Jackie waited for Reed's return, the more tears invaded her eyes and coursed down her cheeks. The death of love. Could their short, glorious time together actually be over? The joy and excitement spilling over her every hour since she'd first met him had vanished, leaving its mementos in pieces. Reed loved her; she'd seen it in his eyes. What had Melanie said to him?

Silence clamored around her like a steeple bell. Her ears echoed his parting words, his reasons for letting her go. He'd fabricated an excuse to stop seeing her; she knew it. His career? She refused to accept his excuse. They were meant to be together, and she felt certain their love came as a gift from God. How could he simply throw it all away?

Jackie slid to the floor and hugged her knees close to her chest. Burying her face, she wept until nothing remained inside but emptiness. Too distressed to pray, she remembered the Holy Spirit interceded to the Father when His children could not utter a word. Finally she forced herself to stand. A shower. . .she'd take a long shower. Then she'd pray and read her Bible. *Why? Oh, Lord, why have You taken Reed away from me?* Somewhere, sometime God would answer her questions.

Sleep escaped Jackie that night. Oh, she tried to numb her wayward thoughts, but instead she reflected upon conversations with Reed, things they'd done together, and places they'd gone. Never had he indicated a problem between them. In fact, he'd stated on numerous occasions how well they fit together. He often claimed God had brought her to him, and he thanked the Father for their precious love. Did Reed feel any remorse over what he'd done?

twenty

Slipping the master key into the door of Jackie's office, Melanie stole inside. All night she'd fought depression and finally near dawn realized how to halt the "monster." Yesterday's escapade had temporarily lifted her spirits, although she was forced to allow Norm to console her. But when Reed failed to call her last night in response to her phone message, she fell to great lows. *He should have called,* she thought, as her desire for revenge spurred her to speed up her scheme. *All he needed to do is phone information for my number and give me his decision.* Except Reed had insisted upon being stubborn. Well, let him keep his little girlfriend. After Melanie completed this morning's maneuver, nothing could save Jackie.

She glanced about her. Norm had already taken his coffee and buried himself in his office after she'd allowed him to kiss her—distasteful, but necessary. Within moments she located Jackie's password, taped on the inside of her top right-hand drawer. The passwords changed monthly, but Melanie had seen where Jackie hid hers during the week of training. After logging into the computer, she quickly began to work. With her mind racing, Melanie set up a general ledger account under Jackie's name using funds from a tax-withholding account. She wanted to use an account not audited as regularly as others, which gave her three to four months to successfully implicate Jackie in embezzling bank funds. Next, Melanie made her coworker's auto loan payment from the new account. *Here's to your silver Camaro,* she thought with a satisfied smile. Melanie planned to initiate at least two more payments from this account before Jackie was discovered. Smiling to herself, Melanie wondered how Reed planned to date a woman behind bars.

Expertly, Melanie logged out and shut down the computer. Locking the office door behind her, she remembered that she hadn't eaten breakfast. A frosted doughnut with little colored candy sprinkles and coffee sounded good this morning.

≈

Early that morning Jackie had risen and taken another shower. She chose a gray pin-striped suit for the day, thinking it befit her mood. Examining her face in the mirror, she added more blush to her wan cheeks and concealer to the dark shadows beneath her eyes. No point in broadcasting her sleepless night to the entire world. As she drove to the bank, she wondered how Melanie would treat her, especially after the previous day's events. She ought to feel pretty chipper, especially since she'd managed to have her own way on two separate occasions. Repeatedly, Jackie told herself to focus on the Problem Solver, not the problem.

≈

Reed glared into the empty computer screen. It had been a long time since he'd despised himself, but today he won the award. He kept remembering the look in Jackie's eyes last night, the hurt and betrayal she relayed to him in a single glance. What a jerk he had been! If only she had screamed at him or thrown him out of her apartment, then possibly he could function this morning. But no, Jackie reacted just like he'd predicted, stuffing her feelings inside to not offend him. No wonder Melanie delighted in taking advantage of her.

His throbbing head and aching neck demanded attention, except he felt like he deserved the pain. It merely matched his heart. Glancing at the clock on his computer he read nine o'clock: time to phone Melanie. Might as well get this over with, too. He called Today's Bank's main number and waited for an answer.

"Melanie Copeland in the real estate loan department," he requested, hating to state her name.

Within moments she came on the line.

"This is Reed," he began, disgust surging through him at the sound of her honeyed voice. "I have a few things to say."

"Why, go right ahead," Melanie replied sweetly. "I expected you to call last night, you naughty man."

He exhaled slowly. "I had things to do. Listen, Melanie, I've broken it off with Jackie. Now, I want your word that you'll leave her alone. She doesn't deserve your tricks."

"Oh, Reed, you want to bargain? Remember, I want you back."

He felt the anger swell in his chest. Barely more than thirty and he was on the verge of a heart attack. "That's not happening," he said tersely. "Jackie is out of the picture, so there's no reason for you to jeopardize her position there at the bank."

"I'll think about it."

"I mean it. I want it stopped."

Melanie laughed lightly. "Are you pleading?"

Reed tightened his jaw and swallowed what little pride he had left. "Yes, I am."

She paused and he contemplated what her ultimatum might be this time. "All right. This will do for now. I'll let you know later what else I may need. Bye, Reed. . .and thanks for the call. You just brightened my day."

Slamming his fist unto the credenza holding his computer, he replaced the phone and spun around to his desk. Nathan stood in the doorway, his arms crossed, wearing a concerned frown.

Reed stared into his friend's face. "You heard?" he asked quietly.

Nathan nodded. "Enough to know Melanie is at it again."

"Yes, she is."

"Would you like to talk?"

He gazed into Nathan's dark blue eyes—so sincere, always a friend when Reed needed one. "Yeah, suppose so. Come on in and take a seat. I'll explain what's been going on. . ."

After he finished, Nathan hesitated before speaking. "The truth is you love Jackie and she loves you, but you're letting Melanie rule you just like she did years ago."

"Do you have a better idea?" Reed asked sarcastically. "Because I'm fresh out."

"No, but I know who does."

Reed pressed his lips together. "I've been talking to God, and I'm waiting for Him to tell me what to do next."

ಇ

The morning inched on at Today's Bank, and despite Jackie's broken heart, she still had a job to perform. A steady stream of customers came and left. She forced a smile and took their applications. Already, she sensed a migraine and as soon as she had a chance, she swallowed her prescribed medication.

Just before noon, Jackie heard a knock on her office door. Thinking it would be another customer, she glanced up to find Melanie leaning against the side of the doorway. As usual, her makeup and dress looked like the front cover of a magazine. Today, she wore an ice blue silk suit. *Ice blue for the ice queen,* Jackie thought bitterly. Immediately, she regretted that thought. *God, forgive me,* she silently prayed. *My pain is no excuse for dishonoring You.*

"You wanted something?" she asked politely.

"Of course," Melanie replied, sauntering inside. "I wondered how you were doing this morning, since Reed is no longer in the picture."

"News travels fast," Jackie said, feeling her heart sink. She hadn't spoken a word about the breakup to anyone.

"It was inevitable, you know. I really wanted him back." Melanie flicked an invisible speck of lint from her shoulder. "We spent last night together. Hmm," she gloated and closed her eyes dreamily, "it had been a long time since we. . .well, you know. At least he ended it with you before he came knocking on my door. My Reed does have ethics."

Jackie formed her words carefully. "If you are finished, you may leave my office. I have work to do."

"Oh, naturally," Melanie replied apologetically. "One more thing, Jackie. Don't ever cross me again. I get what I want, when I want, and how I want it. Remember that. I'm out of your league—always have been." She hurled her words at Jackie with a triumphant glare. "You lose. I win. The name of the game."

Jackie watched Melanie slink down the hallway. Undeniably, the woman looked gorgeous, like a Greek goddess. Too bad she had to resort to such evil manipulations. An inkling of doubt slithered into her mind about Reed. Melanie knew all about last night. How could she, unless he really went to see her?

I will not believe the worst about him, she thought stubbornly. *This is simply more of Melanie's delusions.*

❧

The days passed as though they were suspended in time. While at work, Jackie kept herself busy, but the evenings and weekends left her feeling hollow. Melanie kept her distance, but she had stopped her tricks. She had Reed, and causing Jackie harm no longer held any allure. Once Wilson Anderson returned from vacation, Jackie explained what happened in Norm's office while he was gone. The vice president failed to respond, which bothered Jackie more than Melanie and Norm's indiscretion. A nudging at her mind told her Norm had already consulted Wilson about the matter. And since it remained Melanie's word against hers, Jackie decided to let it rest. She had enough to consider with mending her broken heart.

Jackie couldn't recall what she did with her free hours before Reed. Now there were no more walks in the park, giggles and kisses, or late nights on the phone to fill the hours. She had felt so sure he had been the right one. Hadn't God indicated His favor on their relationship? Maybe she wanted it so badly that she ignored the warnings signs. But nothing had ever indicated a problem, until the night Reed ended it all. Finally Jackie crept to the love and acceptance of her family. No one asked about Reed, and she didn't offer any information. Praise God for such a dear, loving family.

Four weeks later, while laboring over a spreadsheet report, Jackie received an unexpected call.

"Jackie? This is Kathi Bennett, Nathan's wife. Remember me?"

Jackie could not forget the vibrant strawberry blond and her instant friendship. A cloud of melancholy sprinkled its dampness on Jackie's spirit. She and Reed had enjoyed spending time with Nathan and Kathi. "Yes, of course. How are you?"

"Oh, fine. The question is, how are you handling things these days?"

Jackie smiled sadly into the phone. "Some days bad, some days horrible."

"Reed's not doing much better."

"Why? He got what he wanted."

"Jackie, he's miserable. He loves you so much."

"But he's back with Melanie—or didn't he tell you why he broke it off?"

"Reed told Nathan and Nathan told me. He's not seeing Melanie. Reed is too smart to ever go back with the likes of her again. All he's doing is working, sitting at home, and attending church."

Jackie sat upright in her chair. She glanced at the secretaries' desks across the hallway. "Hold on a minute, Kathi. I want to shut my office door." Seconds later, she picked up the phone again. "I don't understand this. Melanie is forever raving about what she and Reed are doing."

"It's all lies. I couldn't decide whether to call you or not, but I know how'd I feel if I was in your position. You see, Reed stopped seeing you because Melanie threatened to do something horrible to you."

Relief brought tears to Jackie's eyes. "I didn't want to think the worst, but with Melanie's continuous flaunting. . ."

"I understand, and I'd have my doubts, too. I want you to know Nathan and I are praying for both of you, and I will tell him tonight about my call."

"What can I do?" Jackie asked, struggling to regain her composure.

"Nothing, except pray for God's justice."

Jackie took a deep breath to stop the flow of any more emotion. "All right," she softly agreed. "Oh, Kathi, I do love Reed. It's so hard without him."

She heard Kathi sniffle. "Now, I'm crying. Just keep praying. Have faith God will work everything out."

twenty-one

Four months crept by while Jackie waited—waited for the pain to ease in her heart while she clung to Kathi Bennett's words of hope. Daily, she prayed for courage and strength until the day Reed returned to her. She found herself pondering the idea of seeking another job, one without Melanie Copeland. A short time ago, Jackie wouldn't have dreamed of leaving Today's Bank, but now she clung to different priorities. Modeling Jesus for Melanie became a passion, although Jackie questioned if her motives were selfish. It didn't matter, because the woman mocked all Jackie's attempts at friendship.

Kathi phoned every other week to check on Jackie. She looked forward to the calls; just hearing news about Reed made her feel closer to him. His home neared completion, but according to Kathi, he'd lost his enthusiasm for the project and contemplated selling it.

"Reed got a promotion this week," Kathi revealed one evening. "He impressed the upper management with his new safety designs."

"Oh, I'm so glad," Jackie said wistfully. "He takes a lot of pride in his work. I'm happy for him."

"Why don't you call and congratulate him?" Kathi suggested. "I'm telling you, he's miserable."

Jackie frowned. "It wouldn't do any good. I don't know about him, but I'd feel worse knowing nothing has changed. I really think Reed should make the first move—after all, he ended the relationship. Besides, if he's not willing to work out a solution where Melanie is concerned, then it's useless."

"Oh, I understand, and I feel sorry for both of you. She destroyed him once and it looks like she's done it again."

Jackie's concern and curiosity heightened; she couldn't

148

help but ask. "Why does Melanie behave this way?"

"Hmm," Kathi replied thoughtfully. "Years ago, after Reed surrendered his life to Jesus, Nathan asked him the same question. At the time, he told us that as a child and a young teen, Melanie got everything she wanted. Her parents provided for her every whim and fancy. When they found the Lord and began living for Him, they changed their parenting techniques and Melanie rebelled. She hated them for refusing to hand out money and purchase expensive gifts. Guess she's been rebelling and running from the Lord ever since."

"How sad." Jackie hesitated, pondering the thought of Melanie as a girl and now an adult. "She must have been difficult to handle, and I feel sorry for her parents. Thanks, Kathi, for telling me; maybe now I can understand her better."

"Sure, you're welcome. I always tell Nathan what we've discussed. He hates the problems between you and Reed as much as I do."

"Both of you are a comfort to me, and I'm glad Reed has friends like you," Jackie replied. "It makes this bearable."

"As I've said before, the Lord will work out the details."

She heard Kathi and Nathan's baby crying in the background. "I'd better let you go; sounds like you're needed. I'll talk to you soon."

Jackie replaced the phone, a bittersweet cloud trailing across her mind. She'd love to talk to Reed, hear his voice, and hold on to a few moments of what they once shared. But she felt too convicted that she should wait on the Lord's timing. Jackie closed her eyes and remembered the first time he had taken her to see his property. He was excited about building his house. She wondered if he stayed with the selections they'd made together. Maybe she could drive by and see the progress. . . No, it would simply hurt too much.

❧

Excitement sped through Melanie as she placed a double payment on Jackie's car loan from the simulated general ledger account. This made six extra installments. The internal auditors were scheduled to review the accounts in three days. Melanie could hardly wait to see the look on Wilson's face when he learned Jackie had embezzled money. Melanie had managed to speak to him alone in his office on a few occasions, most recently yesterday afternoon.

"The real estate applications keep piling up," she'd said, lacing her words with sweetness. "I worry the customers may take their business to another lending institution."

"We do need to get caught up," he'd confirmed as she admired his finely chiseled features.

She watched the light shining through his window reflect on his thick sandy-colored hair. She couldn't wait to have him in her clutches.

"Are you offering to help?" Melanie asked shyly.

Wilson gave her a cordial smile. "I don't think so. Have you talked to Jackie or Norm?"

Melanie laughed lightly. "Yes, I have; Norm's swamped and Jackie refuses."

He raised a brow in disbelief. "Possibly you misinterpreted her reply. I'll mention to her that you need assistance."

Melanie shook her head. "No, Wilson, please. I'm not one of her favorite people, and it's difficult enough working in the same area."

"I see," he replied, his deep blue eyes studying her face. "So the problems between you two haven't been resolved?"

"Not yet. I apologize for complaining, and I'll get caught up." She rose from her chair, indicating a desire to get back to work. Proffering a smile, she added, "But you can help me if you like." Without waiting for a response, she exited Wilson's office, making sure to greet Carla as she left.

Now seated at her desk, Melanie realized she'd soon have Wilson Anderson in the palm of her hand, just like all the other men who found her desirable.

Giggling, she glanced at the time on her computer. Only four more hours until she saw Reed. She had the evening planned and memorized. The walk-through inspection for his new house had been scheduled at seven-thirty, and although he'd refused to see her before, tonight he had no choice.

Reed walked Yukon through the familiar paths around the apartment complex. Disgruntled and lonely without Jackie, he was in a surly mood. He dreaded meeting Melanie at the new house. He didn't want her near the place. After all, it was supposed to have been for him and Jackie. Even with the contractor in attendance, Reed flinched at the thought of the evening.

He kept thinking Melanie would soon grow tired of her little games, but she still called him regularly. He'd gotten to the point of not answering the phone at all. Now she left lengthy messages on his answering machine.

Reed shook his head at the despair winding through him. If he thought for one minute Melanie wanted his house, he'd give it to her tonight. Anything to make her leave him alone. Somehow he didn't think Jackie would mind where they lived—if she'd still have him. He knew Kathi kept in touch with her, and somehow Kathi's friendship with Jackie comforted him. Staring up into the late afternoon sky laced with shades of deeper blue, Reed thought how long it had been since he gazed into Jackie's hazel eyes or heard her voice. So many times he'd picked up the phone to call, but he couldn't. At least, not yet.

Finishing his walk with Yukon, he meandered back toward his apartment. While he fed his dog, he glanced at the answering machine and expelled a grateful breath. Melanie hadn't left one of her disgusting messages.

Lord, help me handle this meeting tonight with wisdom and discernment, he prayed. *I cannot lose my temper, or she will win one more time.*

At seven o'clock, Reed slid into the driver's seat of his Blazer and headed out of town. He purposely intended to be over ten minutes late so the contractor would already be there. All the way to the house, he thought about Jackie. Oh, how he prayed God would work out a way for them to be reunited.

As he drove the lengthy driveway to his house tucked away in the trees, he saw Melanie's little black sports car. Unfortunately, he realized he must face her alone, because no other vehicles were parked outside; the contractor must have come and gone. Taking a moment to study the magnificent home, he felt a mixture of pride and sadness. Jackie should have been seated beside him, and they could have inspected the workmanship together while planning their future.

Grabbing a notepad and pen from the truck seat, he made his way to the front entrance. Opening the wood-paneled, double doors, he stepped onto the ivory and tan tile of the two-story foyer. He couldn't help but appreciate the pleasing sights and fresh smells of the new construction. A living room stood to his right and a dining room to his left. Although he wanted Jackie beside him, he still admired the cream-colored walls and pecan hardwood floors. The contractor had suggested the cove molding and eleven-foot ceilings, and Reed took the advice. Every room held upgrades, either in the way of wood trim, flooring, or lighting and plumbing fixtures. Without taking another step, he knew this house needed two people to call it a home—him and Jackie.

"Reed, is that you?" Melanie called from somewhere on the first floor.

Apprehensive of being alone with her, Reed walked straight through to a large family room that hosted a stone, double-walled fireplace adjoined by the kitchen.

"There you are," she replied sweetly from the breakfast area. "You're late, sweetheart, and I have so much planned for tonight."

Irritated at the sound of her syrupy voice, he stated resolutely, "Is the contractor coming back?"

Melanie laughed lightly. "It doesn't matter. We don't need him. Come look at the surprise I have for you."

Reluctantly, Reed ventured toward the kitchen. The faint aroma of spices and pasta perked his attention. Instantly he spotted a beige linen tablecloth on the tiled floor of the breakfast area. Melanie had set it with fine china and crystal. On the opposite end of the table settings rested several dishes from a local, exclusive Italian restaurant. His gaze flew to

Melanie, dressed in a candy-apple-red, long, snug gown. Diamond jewelry glittered from her ears and throat. In each hand she carried a wineglass, filled to the brim with the fruit of the vine. Offering him one of the drinks, she bestowed a brazen smile through bloodred lipstick.

"What is this?" he demanded, his irritation rising. "We have a business arrangement here tonight, nothing else. And where is Jim?"

"Oh," Melanie cooed, "he had another appointment, so it's just you and me." She moved toward him, seductively tempting him to take the wine.

Reed shook his head. The scent of her expensive perfume filled his nostrils. "Melanie, I'm not interested, either in the wine or you. Why don't you stop before you make a fool out of yourself?"

"I know you still care for me." She inched closer.

"Yes, I care about you, but not in the way you think or want."

Her smile faltered. "What do you mean?"

"I mean I care about your heart, your soul. Nothing would please me more than to see you turn your life over to Jesus Christ."

Melanie rolled her eyes. "Oh, it's the religion thing again."

Reed took a deep breath, filled with pity for the woman before him. "Melanie, you know the truth—your parents taught you about the Lord."

"I don't need a crutch or a stupid list of rules."

"Jesus is neither. He loves you and wants you to surrender your life to Him."

Melanie's ice blue eyes glared angrily at him. She took another step and threw the glass of wine on his face and down his shirt. "That's what I think of you and your God."

"Why?" he asked softly. "Why is it so hard for you to see Jesus loves you?"

"Shut up, Reed. I've gone to a lot of trouble for tonight, and you're spoiling my party." She trembled with rage and clenched her fists.

"Then I'll leave you alone," he stated calmly. "I'll call the bank in the morning and request that someone else handle my walk-through."

"Such as Jackie?"

"No, I'm sure there are other capable employees." He turned and walked through the house toward the front door.

"Don't you dare walk out on me!" Melanie screamed. "I'll destroy you; I know how. And I'll set fire to this house of yours."

Reed chose not to reply, but merely closed the door and made his way to the truck. He picked up his cell phone and phoned the police.

Reed gave them the address of his location and the circumstances. "Yes, sir. It seems the woman representing my bank is here and is threatening to burn my house. I'd simply like to have her escorted from the property."

While he waited for the patrol car to arrive, he wiped the wine from his face and shirt. He hoped Melanie would leave on her own, but by the time the officers arrived, she still had not left the house.

"Officer, this is merely a lovers' quarrel and not an issue for you," she insisted when the policeman questioned her.

"Perhaps a call to the contractor would clear up the matter," Reed suggested.

A few moments later, a police officer spoke with the contractor. Once the home's ownership had been established, Melanie angrily handed Reed the house keys and hurried to her sports car.

After thanking the officers, Reed drove toward Toledo. Feeling amazingly in control, he came to a startling revelation. He wanted to see Jackie. Reed loved her with all his heart, and if she would take him back, then they'd find a way out of this dilemma. Melanie's little stunt tonight had proved one thing. She held no power over him, not as long as he held onto the hand of God.

twenty-two

All the way to Jackie's, Reed rehearsed what he should say. "How are you? Job going okay?" *Fool, she ought to slap you.* "I love you, Jackie, and I'm sorry." *No, that's not good enough.* "I'm sorry I hurt you; will you forgive me?" *I need something more sincere.* "Can we talk? There are a few things I'd like to say." He pounded his palm against his head. Why should he fret about what to say to her? Hadn't God seen him through the bad times in the past? Hadn't He helped him tonight with Melanie? And hadn't God led him to go see Jackie?

Oh, Lord, I'm acting like a kid instead of a grown man. I praise You for Your guidance. You know I've never been much on words, and I don't have any idea how to present things so Jackie will listen, but You do. Untangle my mind, Father. You are my ever-present help. Amen.

Taking a deep breath, Reed glanced down at the speedometer and eased his foot off the accelerator. He surely didn't want a ticket tonight. Slowly, his mind ceased to race and by the time he pulled into Jackie's apartment complex, he'd calmed considerably.

As he stepped out of the Blazer and took a quick glimpse at the second-story window of her living room, he saw the drapes were drawn. Hopefully, she hadn't closed her mind, too. Shoving his keys into his jeans pocket, Reed ascended the stairs.

Anchored in front of her door, his knees suddenly felt weak. He shook his head to dispel the fear and lifted his fist to knock—hard. The knob turned and suddenly Reed couldn't remember his own name.

"Hi," he managed, when Jackie opened the door. She looked incredibly beautiful, her hazel eyes wide in surprise and her cheeks faintly flushed. She wore a burnt orange sundress, and her dark curls were tied at the crown of her head in a long ponytail. "I can understand if you're busy, but I'd like to talk."

Jackie nibbled at her lower lip as though not certain how to respond.

"Do you have company?" Reed asked, a detail he hadn't imagined.

"No," she replied after a moment. When he rested his gaze upon hers, she hastily turned away. "I'm sorry; what did you say?"

"I said I'd like to talk, if you don't mind."

She nodded slowly. "Okay. Did you want to come in?"

He glanced at the wine-stained tip of his right tennis shoe. "I don't want to make you feel uncomfortable. We can sit outside, if that's easier."

Jackie hesitated, and Reed couldn't blame her. He knew he'd hurt her badly, and he deserved to have the door shut in his face.

"What about a bench near the pool?" she suggested.

"Sounds good to me." Relief poured from his soul.

She gathered up her keys and followed him outside and down the stairs. Reed mentioned the warm weather and asked if she'd used the pool much this summer. Surface talk. . .small talk, until they reached a secluded bench. She sat on one end and he on the other, as stiff as diplomats from warring countries.

Evening shadows quickly closed in from a navy blue sky. He welcomed the comfort of darkness to hide his restlessness, but then he couldn't see Jackie's eyes. Her emotions had always risen and fallen in those hazel pools, a sign of what surfaced inside her.

"Have you been drinking?" she asked unexpectedly.

He remembered Melanie's fit of anger. "No, not at all. You smell the wine Melanie threw at me tonight." He quickly explained what had transpired at the house.

"So what made you decide to come see me?" she asked, barely above a whisper.

He wanted to reach for her hand but thought better of it. Instead he turned to face her. A torchlight from an apartment behind her haloed her hair.

"I'm not sure where to start. When I told you I loved you, I meant it. I wanted us to last. . .well, forever. You were—and are—an important part of my life. Then, out of desperation over the things happening to you at work, I hurt you. Jackie, I never intended to do that. I wanted you safe. . .protected from anything or anyone who might cause you harm."

"You thought by breaking it off with me, Melanie would stop her tricks?"

"Yes," he replied simply.

"Did you go back to her?"

She looked so hurt, and it tore at his heart. "No, I hadn't seen or talked with her until about an hour ago when we met at the house for the final walk-through."

Jackie nodded. "She told me."

Reed took a deep breath. "I realized tonight the only power Melanie has over me is what I give her. She's pathetic and lost. In fact, I told her this evening she needs Jesus."

"Obviously she disagreed."

Silence reigned until he found the courage to continue. "Jackie, if you will have me, I want you back. I love you, and I'm willing to do about anything to make things right between us, but it has to be your decision."

His only answer was the quiet sounds of singing insects and the distant voices from other apartments; he nearly gave up.

"Reed, I never stopped loving you," she began at last, her words edged with emotion, "and though I understand why you walked away from me, you never gave me enough credit to believe I could stand up to Melanie. We could have fought her together. I've often wondered if I should have shared with you all those things that happened."

"I wanted to help," he interrupted. "I needed to help you. But now I see we must communicate openly and honestly if we are to make this relationship work. . .if you want it to last."

"I want it to work," she murmured with a soft sob.

Reed didn't know who reached out first, but suddenly they were in each other's arms, holding on to make up for all those weeks they'd been apart. He heard her muffled weeping and felt the dampness on her cheeks. For a moment he feared his joy would turn into tears.

Hours later, they still sat entwined on the bench, neither willing to part.

"I don't care what Melanie does," Jackie stated stubbornly.

"She can make your job so difficult," he warned, brushing a loose curl from her face. "And she will be out for revenge after I called the police tonight."

"If I can't find a way to bring her deception to Wilson's attention, then I'll look for employment elsewhere."

"But you love your position at the bank," he softly protested.

"Not as much as I love you," she replied, reaching up to touch his face.

As they sealed their renewed commitment with a lingering kiss, Reed felt a sense of foreboding. "Let's pray," he said. "We need God's blessings and protection more than ever."

In the blackness of night, beneath a sliver of a moon, Reed prayed for the two of them.

૨ક

Readying herself for work the following morning, Jackie couldn't remember such contentment. God had answered her prayers, and this time for keeps. Jackie and Reed had talked long past midnight, working through the problems about Melanie and setting goals for the future. The road ahead seemed hopeful, even with the trouble Melanie would surely cause.

"She's angry," Reed had warned, "and she can't be trusted."

"How ironic," Jackie commented reflectively. "Once she told me to beware of your temper."

"Oh?" he questioned. "I admit to having problems controlling it in the past. What did she say?"

"That you and she were involved in a car accident as a result of your anger, and she had a scar to prove it."

Reed whistled. "Melanie sure knows how to twist the

truth. Let me tell you what really happened. We were on our way to a party and had a terrible argument. She got so mad that she unfastened her seat belt, started beating her fists into my face, then grabbed the steering wheel. I lost control of the car, and it sliced a telephone pole. She fell sideways into the dashboard and received a nasty cut on her right thigh. So, yes, we were involved in an accident, and yes, she does have a scar to prove it. Her fabrications never cease to amaze me."

Jackie could only stare at him incredulously. "How can Melanie make up these things?"

"I'm not sure," he replied. "But I do think she believes her own lies."

"How sad," Jackie whispered, "and I will be careful. Now I know her capabilities, which helps. If I could only figure out how she got into my office and got access to my computer."

"Honey," Reed said, pulling her into his arms, "if there's a way, Melanie will find it. All she needed was a key and a password."

"And all we need is to find out how she got both of them."

Once more, as Jackie pulled into a parking space at the bank, she felt a chill race up her spine. What would she say if she walked in on Melanie going through her office?

As she climbed the steps of the bank building, Jackie caught sight of Wilson and Norm walking in together. A twinge of nervousness swept through her as she remembered the unpleasant scene in Norm's office—the last episode of Melanie's troublemaking. Wilson had treated her rather coolly since then, and Jackie suspected Melanie had something to do with that, too. Norm openly eyed her with contempt; she'd come to expect his scowls.

I haven't done anything to feel uncomfortable around them, she told herself and decided to wait at the top of the steps for the two men. "Good morning," Jackie greeted with a smile.

Norm muttered something about the day being hot, but Wilson returned the gesture and opened the door for her.

"Thank you," she said, "and have a good day."

As she hurried toward her office, she heard Norm say,

"The situation is intolerable, and I'm afraid we're going to lose a valuable employee."

Jackie shivered. Her imagination must be running wild. Norm must have gone to Wilson with all of Melanie's complaints.

The morning progressed normally, and at noon she had lunch with Reed. He met her in the lobby of the Oaken Bucket.

"Is Melanie behaving herself?" he asked with a worried frown.

"Yes. In fact, I haven't seen much of her today."

"Good. I phoned your supervisor, Norm Timmons, this morning and requested a different bank representative for my walk-through. When he asked why, I told him I had a personality conflict with Melanie Copeland."

"What did he say?"

Reed shook his head. "Nothing. We scheduled it for tomorrow afternoon." He planted a light kiss on her cheek. "I wanted you with me, but it's at two o'clock."

She tilted her head and gave him a smile. "You're sweet, but the closing is next week, right?" When he nodded, she continued, "You can give me my own private tour then."

He grinned and the two entered the restaurant hand in hand. Jackie relished his company. All those weeks she'd lived on memories. . .hoping and praying that they would be reunited. Now, as he held tightly to her hand, she wanted to pinch herself to make sure it wasn't all a dream.

❧

Reed leafed through his mail, humming some nondescript tune. The walk-through had gone nicely. This time Jim, the contractor, attended along with Norm Timmons. Reed had listed a few items that needed attention, and Jim agreed to have them completed by closing next week.

Mr. Timmons had acted as though he'd made a big concession by representing the real estate loan department. Reed couldn't help but observe that neither his appearance nor his professional facade fit Melanie's style. Reed concluded she must be using him. Norm kept glancing at his watch and referring to Miss Copeland as the best real estate loan officer in the business. Reed chose to ignore him. No point in starting an argument where he might make working conditions more difficult for Jackie.

The phone rang, interrupting his thoughts about the afternoon. "Hi, Reed. I just wanted to tell you that it's not over yet. Things are not always what they seem." *Click.*

Melanie, can't you simply give up? he inwardly moaned. He remembered Jackie telling him she wanted to look for another job. Somehow her decision didn't set right with him. She had an excellent position at Today's Bank, and she enjoyed the people—most of them, anyway. Melanie should be the one beating the streets for new employment.

With a heavy sigh, he glanced at his watch and saw he had an hour until taking Jackie to a movie. Just enough time to stop at a few jewelry stores. . .

twenty-three

The following morning as Jackie met with a customer about a new auto application, Wilson called.

"Can you come to my office?" he asked.

Jackie detected a strange ring to his voice. "I'm with a customer. . ."

"Get one of the secretaries to finish it," Wilson replied curtly.

"All right." Jackie shivered and hung up the phone.

With the customer in the care of a capable secretary, Jackie headed to see Wilson. She didn't like the sound of his voice—not one bit.

Once inside his office, she saw the two internal auditors seated near his desk.

"Come in, Jackie, and shut the door," Wilson instructed, pointing to an empty chair. His attention seemed to be drawn to the computer.

Sending up a prayer, she sat near the auditors. "What is this about?" she asked, hoping no one picked up on her trepidation.

Wilson leaned back and eyed her curiously. "Do you know how many payments are left on your car loan?"

Taken back by his unusual request, Jackie mentally calculated the months remaining. "Thirteen."

Unwavering in his look, Wilson replied, "The records show seven."

"That's impossible," she replied, confused.

"Would you like to see for yourself?" He turned the computer screen toward her.

Jackie saw the payment schedule. "It says I have made six extra payments in the last three months, but I haven't." She looked around the small room, first to the man and woman who were internal auditors and then to Wilson. "This is wrong," she pointed out. "I have thirteen payments remaining on my car."

Wilson picked up his pen, then laid it back down on his desk. The lines etched across his forehead indicated a problem. . .a serious problem. "Jackie, the auditors have discovered you have taken money from an income tax withholding account, set up a general ledger account, and proceeded to make extra payments on your car."

"That's not true! I would never. . ."

"It was done from your computer with your password," Wilson said flatly.

Jackie felt the panic rising through her veins. "But I didn't do it."

Wilson wet his lips. "I'm sorry, Jackie, but I will have to call a security guard to escort you from the bank. We will be in contact with you about the problem."

She instantly rose from her chair and stared at him, dumbfounded. "But you are accusing me of embezzlement!"

Wilson hesitated. "Believe me, I am shocked at this. I would never have suspected you of anything underhanded, but the evidence is quite clear."

Utterly humiliated, Jackie could only fight back the tears. So Melanie had struck again. "I will find a way to prove I didn't do this," she said as calmly as her quivering lips permitted.

Turning, she saw the security guard in the outer office. Without another word, she accompanied him downstairs. Jackie felt everyone's eyes piercing through her, but she steadied her gaze straight ahead. Her head pounded, promising a migraine, and she thought her shaky knees would give way. *Oh, Lord, I'm so scared,* she prayed. *Thieves go to jail; even those falsely accused, provided there is evidence to convict them.* Suddenly, Melanie stepped out in front of her. She moved to allow Jackie to walk by, but not without showing a faint smirk.

Jackie retrieved her purse and allowed the guard to escort her to her car—the car with only seven payments left on the balance.

Jackie sat on the white leather sofa of her apartment, numb, too emotionally drained to do anything but stare blankly at a Picasso reproduction on the opposite wall. She'd called Reed, and he was on his way. So all she could do was wait, something she'd not mastered well. Once she considered calling an attorney, but who? A criminal lawyer? And her parents deserved to know what happened. They wouldn't want her to be alone. Jackie sighed. She didn't want to be alone either. She wanted Reed.

The burden of the day weighed heavily on her mind and heart. Melanie had found a way to get into her office and locate her password, but how? And how would Jackie ever prove it? It looked like an impossibility—except God worked miracles. He knew the truth, and He knew she hadn't taken a dime from the bank.

Utterly devastated, Jackie lowered her head and whispered, "Heavenly Father, I'm frightened. It really looks like I have embezzled money. Help me clear my name of these lies. My desire is not to have people punished, but for the truth to be known. And, Lord, Melanie needs You."

In a short while, Reed arrived and urged her to cuddle with him on the sofa. For several minutes he simply held her close.

"All of this is wrong, unfair, and I can't help but feel responsible," he said. She heard the guilt in his voice. "Honey, I'm so sorry about today—and all the other times she's hurt you."

"I won't be defeated," Jackie whispered. "I refuse to give in to this." She paused. "I know God is for us, and the Bible says we Christians will face persecution, but I never expected anything like what has happened."

Reed stroked her hair as though she were a small child in his arms. "We never are quite ready for the trials of life. Remember when you told me about focusing on the Problem Solver and not the problem?" Jackie nodded and he continued, "He sustained me through those months without you, and our Lord will be our strength now."

"I keep telling myself the same thing. Reed, don't feel like you have to stick with me through this. It could be very nasty, especially with the evidence piled against me." Jackie pulled away from his chest. "I don't want to jeopardize your. . ."

He silenced her by touching his fingers to her lips. "You're stuck with me, pretty lady. Whatever happens—and I firmly believe in God's sovereignty—we will see this to the end together."

"I love you," she whispered, gazing into his brown eyes.

Smiling, he kissed her lightly, and she relaxed in his arms.

"We should drive out to your parents," he stated a moment later. "They will want to help."

Jackie breathed deeply. "You're right. If only I could spare them the heartache."

Reed lifted her chin. "This is not a solo project, but a labor of love for all of us who care about you. We can pray together and see what God will have us do next."

She toyed with a wayward curl. "Let's go now before I lose my courage."

Reed stood and helped Jackie to her feet. She treasured his encouragement and quiet strength.

❧

As the tires hummed along the highway to Ron and Nita's, Reed's mind spun. The two of them rode in silence, absorbed in their own thoughts. *Tell me, Lord. Show me what to do,* he prayed. Frustration swelled inside him as overwhelming helplessness threatened to take control.

"I thought of contacting a lawyer," Jackie finally said, breaking the stillness, "except I didn't know who to call. The bank could easily file felony charges against me."

Reed took a quick glimpse at her pale face. The sight of her visibly upset sent fury through every inch of him. Sighing, he reached over for her hand. It felt cold and clammy. "I've been thinking. I'd like, with your permission, to set up an appointment with Wilson Anderson."

"What would that accomplish?" she asked, turning to face him. "You can't prove those messages left on your answering machine were from Melanie, can you?"

"Of course I can. I saved them all, and in some she identified herself. I can record those messages to play for Wilson or anyone else who will listen." He paused reflectively. "I'd also like to call the locksmith company to see if their servicemen log in and out. She may have had enough time that day to copy the master key before giving it to Wilson's secretary."

Jackie nodded slowly. "As far as my password, Melanie may have seen mine taped to the back of my desk drawer. Those are changed once a month, but I still keep the new word in the same place. In fact, I remember referring to it when I trained her."

"All definite possibilities," he concluded. "Have you ever considered it odd how Melanie moved from the big city to Toledo? Chicago is full of banks, and she isn't much for small towns."

"Well, she certainly expressed her dissatisfaction with Toledo. She said our fair city bores her."

"My point," Reed replied, "and she has yet to phone her parents. Has she ever indicated why she left Chicago?"

Jackie shook her dark head. "Truthfully, I've wondered about her transfer, but I don't have any answers."

"The reasons may be what we need to get to the truth."

Jackie looked puzzled. "But how can you find out?"

He forced a faint smile. "I probably can't, but Wilson definitely could make some calls."

Reed felt certain of his direction. In recalling his dealings with Melanie eight years ago, she had a history of destroying lives. While they were engaged, she had been involved with a married man. At the time, Reed refused to acknowledge the affair. However, the same day she broke their engagement, Melanie strode into their favorite restaurant arm in arm with another man. Reed really doubted her lifestyle had changed much while living in Chicago.

&

Jackie clicked off the lamp on her nightstand and snuggled between the sheets. She knew sleep would evade her, so she chose to use this time to put some sort of meaning into the inextricable day. The circumstances involving her dismissal from Today's Bank held her spellbound somewhere in the zone between shame and fury. The fact she could not prove her innocence left a sick, helpless feeling in the pit of her stomach.

What would she ever do without the Lord? In the midst of all the misgivings, she felt His hand upon her shoulder. And when Reed assured her of His provision, Jackie trusted in that promise. *Oh, Father, thank You for sending Reed back to me. I know if need be I could make it through this ordeal without him, but his presence is a comforting reflection of You.*

Smiling into the darkness, Jackie recalled her father's response to the day's events. He'd bellowed and roared like a mighty lion over what had happened to his daughter. Once he calmed himself, he gathered the family together for prayer. There in the kitchen, he asked God to give Jackie guidance and courage. Her mother wept before becoming angry. Jackie's siblings had been wonderful. How did she ever deserve such a loving family?

Jackie sighed and closed her eyes. Maybe she could sleep, after all.

❧

Anxious and tense, Reed waited for Wilson Anderson to complete his phone call. He'd taken a personal day to meet with the vice president and hopefully convince him to investigate Melanie's background. The two men had barely begun their conversation before an urgent call demanded Wilson's attention.

"No media," Wilson stated firmly into the phone. "Under no circumstances are they to speak with any personnel." He paused, his eyes narrowing. "When I find out how they learned about this, someone will be minus a job." Another moment passed until he replaced the receiver.

Wilson forced a smile. "I'm sorry. Seems like I've lost my temper too many times lately." With a heavy sigh, he continued, "As I just stated, I don't want to believe Jackie took those funds, but I don't have any evidence otherwise."

Reed nodded. "I agree it doesn't look good for her, but

when I finish telling you about Melanie, you may have a new perspective." He spent the next several minutes explaining his relationship with Melanie—past and present. "I have a tape of the phone messages threatening Jackie and me." Reed pulled the tape from his pocket and laid it on Wilson's desk. "I also recommend you contact the Chicago bank branch and find out exactly why she transferred here."

Wilson appeared to study the man before him. He leaned back in his chair and folded his hands across his middle. Worry lines settled around his eyes.

"Ask yourself, when did the problems start?" Reed asked.

"All right," Wilson finally agreed, "I'll make a few calls."

"That's all I can ask," Reed replied.

Wilson stood. He looked exhausted. "I'm willing to do whatever is necessary to clear up this unfortunate incident. Jackie has always been a prized employee, one who had a great future with the bank, and I'm sure she appreciates what you are doing for her. I'll be in touch." He shook Reed's hand and the two men parted.

As Reed proceeded to exit the bank building, Melanie suddenly appeared at his side.

"There's nothing you can do to help your ex-girlfriend," she said sweetly.

He glanced at Melanie's black-and-gold pin-striped designer suit and perfectly styled blond hair. "Jackie is not my ex-girlfriend," he replied, fixing his gaze on the double glass doors. "And there's plenty I can do." Without giving her another look, he pushed open the door and headed down the steps to the parking lot.

Climbing into his red Blazer, Reed decided he'd take Jackie to her parents. Surrounded by her family, he anticipated their love and encouragement would help her through the day. In his opinion, Jackie shouldn't be alone, especially if someone chose to alert the media about the previous day's activities. Reed prayed Wilson contacted the Chicago office today.

❧

The following afternoon Reed and Jackie sat in Wilson's

office, waiting for him to return from an earlier meeting. Reed held her hand; it was cold and damp, yet she'd pasted a smile on her face. He could only imagine how difficult it was for her to enter the bank.

"Sorry to keep you waiting," Wilson said, entering his office and seating himself near them. He looked relaxed, satisfied, and amazingly content. "First of all, I want to thank both of you for agreeing to this appointment. Jackie, the past two days must seem like a nightmare to you, and I apologize."

Reed felt his hopes heighten, and he squeezed her hand. Surely God had answered their prayers.

"Reed, I did take your advice yesterday. Not only did I learn of the trouble Melanie caused in Chicago, but I got the information straight from the president of the bank. She had attempted to blackmail him, but he refused to give in to her bargaining techniques. As a result, Melanie had a choice of taking a transfer or losing her job." Wilson sighed. "Recently, he confessed to his wife about the affair with Melanie. My call prompted him to offer his help to us here."

Reed felt Jackie's hand tremble beneath his grasp. He gave her a reassuring smile before Wilson continued.

"This morning, I called Melanie into my office with the internal auditors as witnesses and confronted her on the problems here at the bank. She denied everything, but when the president of the bank from Chicago walked into my office, she was trapped and eventually confessed to everything."

"Praise God," Jackie uttered. "I don't see how she managed to do it all."

Wilson shook his head. "Melanie's brilliant. . .and cunning. Unfortunately, her greed cost her a job, and she may face felony charges."

"What was her goal in all of this?" Reed asked curiously.

Wilson gave him a wry smile. "Money. She had her sights set on pulling the same stunt as in Chicago, but she never expected the people involved to be Christians."

Jackie gazed at Reed appreciatively. "We all had God on our side. I wonder what will happen to her now."

"With the information I received from Reed, I took the liberty of phoning her parents. They were waiting for her when she left my office," Wilson replied.

"How's Norm?" Jackie asked. "I can't help but feel sorry for him."

Wilson expelled a deep breath. "Well, he realized he'd been used. He resigned, but I asked him to reconsider. He has the potential to be a good man."

Jackie nodded in agreement. "He needs Jesus."

"Don't we all?" Wilson agreed. "What about you, Jackie? Will you come back to work for us?"

Jackie nibbled at her lip. "Yes, I'd like to." She smiled. "Looks like I'll have a double position for awhile again."

"I promise you help this time," Wilson stated. "Thank you for your understanding. I know that sounds trite, but I'm so glad all of this is over."

As Jackie and Reed said their good-byes, Wilson grasped Reed's hand firmly. "You're a good man, Reed, a man after God's own heart."

≈

Yukon raced toward Jackie as the Frisbee sailed over his head and straight into her hands. Laughing, she bent to pat the dog affectionately. A small white plastic bag attached to his collar drew her attention. She remembered Reed spending extra time with his pet the last time she sent the Frisbee his way. Carefully she removed the bag from Yukon's collar. At the sight of the tiny black velvet box inside, she began to shake. Enclosed was a folded sheet of paper. With trembling fingers she opened it and read:

> *Jackie,*
> *God has given us the gift of love. I don't want to ever let you go. Will you share my life with me? I love you, and I'm asking you to marry me.*
>
> *Reed*

She felt her pulse race as she lifted the cover of the box. Inside, a diamond solitaire sparkled. She stood up and waved wildly at him. "Yes!" she shouted.

Reed cupped his hand over his ear, indicating that he couldn't hear her.

"Yes!"

Again he cupped his hand over his ear. Jackie sensed his teasing and ran toward him. "Yes, yes, yes," she cried, rushing into Reed's arms. "Tomorrow, I'll marry you tomorrow."

He kissed her lightly, then more deeply as her laughter turned to joyous tears.

"Let your light so shine before men,
that they may see your good works,
and glorify your Father which is in heaven."
MATTHEW 5:16

Introducing a brand new historical novella collection
with four female lighthouse
keepers, at four different points
of the compass in the United
States. Each woman will need to
learn to trust in God and the
guidance of His Light as they
seek to do their appointed tasks.
Salting their characters' lives with
romance, the authors bring each
of these tales to an expected yet
miraculous ending.

When Love Awaits by Lynn A. Coleman
A Beacon in the Storm by Andrea Boeshaar
Whispers Across the Blue by DiAnn Mills
A Time to Love by Sally Laity

paperback, 452 pages, 5 ³⁄₁₆" x 8"

A Letter To Our Readers

Dear Reader:

In order that we might better contribute to your reading enjoyment, we would appreciate your taking a few minutes to respond to the following questions. We welcome your comments and read each form and letter we receive. When completed, please return to the following:

Rebecca Germany, Fiction Editor
Heartsong Presents
PO Box 719
Uhrichsville, Ohio 44683

1. Did you enjoy reading *The Color of Love?*
   ❑ Very much. I would like to see more books
      by this author!
   ❑ Moderately
      I would have enjoyed it more if _____

   _____

   _____

2. Are you a member of **Heartsong Presents**? Yes ❑ No ❑
   If no, where did you purchase this book? _____

   _____

3. How would you rate, on a scale from 1 (poor) to 5 (superior), the cover design? _____

4. On a scale from 1 (poor) to 10 (superior), please rate the following elements.

   _____ Heroine   _____ Plot

   _____ Hero   _____ Inspirational theme

   _____ Setting   _____ Secondary characters

5. These characters were special because_____

_____

_____

6. How has this book inspired your life?_____

_____

_____

7. What settings would you like to see covered in future
   Heartsong Presents books?_____

_____

_____

8. What are some inspirational themes you would like to see
   treated in future books?_____

_____

_____

9. Would you be interested in reading other **Heartsong
   Presents** titles?   Yes ❑   No ❑

10. Please check your age range:
    ❑ Under 18   ❑ 18-24   ❑ 25-34
    ❑ 35-45   ❑ 46-55   ❑ Over 55

11. How many hours per week do you read?_____

Name _____

Occupation _____

Address _____

City _____ State _____ Zip _____

Experience a family

saga that begins in 1860 when the painting of a homestead is first given to a young bride who leaves her beloved home of Laurelwood. Then follow the painting through a legacy of love that touches down in the years 1890, 1969, and finally today. Authors Sally Laity, Andrea Boeshaar, Yvonne Lehman, and DiAnn Mills have worked together to create a timeless treasure of four novellas in one collection.

paperback, 352 pages, 5 ³⁄₁₆" x 8"

❤ ❤ ❤ ❤ ❤ ❤ ❤ ❤ ❤ ❤ ❤ ❤ ❤ ❤ ❤ ❤ ❤

❤ ❤ ❤ ❤ ❤ ❤ ❤ ❤ ❤ ❤ ❤ ❤ ❤ ❤ ❤ ❤ ❤

Heart♥ng Presents
Love Stories
Are Rated G!

That's for godly, gratifying, and of course, great! If you love a thrilling love story, but don't appreciate the sordidness of some popular paperback romances, **Heartsong Presents** is for you. In fact, **Heartsong Presents** is the *only inspirational romance book club* featuring love stories where Christian faith is the primary ingredient in a marriage relationship.

Sign up today to receive your first set of four, never before published Christian romances. Send no money now; you will receive a bill with the first shipment. You may cancel at any time without obligation, and if you aren't completely satisfied with any selection, you may return the books for an immediate refund!

Imagine. . .four new romances every four weeks—two historical, two contemporary—with men and women like you who long to meet the one God has chosen as the love of their lives. . . all for the low price of $9.97 postpaid.

To join, simply complete the coupon below and mail to the address provided. **Heartsong Presents** romances are rated G for another reason: They'll arrive *Godspeed!*